THE HOUSE OF IDEAS

The House Of Ideas
Copyright © 2024 by Mark Pracht

THE HOUSE OF IDEAS

A PLAY BY
MARK PRACHT

PART THREE OF THE FOUR-COLOR TRILOGY

Dedication

COLENE, MY ETERNAL SUNSHINE,
MY ROZ AND JOAN ALL IN ONE.

AND TERRY, WHO TOOK THE LEAP.

THE HOUSE OF IDEAS was originally produced at City Lit Theatre in Chicago, IL from Aug 23rd to Oct 6th, 2024. It was directed by Terry McCabe, produced by Artistic Director Brian Pastor. The Stage Manager was Hazel Flowers-McCabe. Scenic, Lighting and Projection Design was by G. "Max" Maxim IV. Costume Design was by Beth Laske-Miller. Original music and sound design was by Petter Wahlback. Props were designed by Jeff Brain. Original artwork was created by Tony Donley.

The original cast was as follows:

STAN LEE - Bryan Breau

JACK KIRBY - Brian Plocharczyk

JOAN LEE - Kate Black-Spence

ROZ KIRBY - Carrie Hardin

THE OBSERVER - Ben Veatch

MARTIN GOODMAN- Brian Parry

CORPORAL PINKERTON/JIM MOONEY/

CARMINE INFANTINO/MAX SCHMID - Sean Harklerode

PRIVATE DUGAN/JACK SCHIFF/

JACK LIEBOWITZ/MENAHEM GOLAN - Chad Wise

FLO STEINBERG/GREER GRANT/SUZIE SUTTON -

Megan Clarke

JOE SIMON/STAN GOLDBERG/NAT FREEDLAND/

JIM SHOOTER - Jimmy Hogan

(THE ROLE OF ROBERT KNIGHT WAS REPLACED WITH MAX SCHMID FOR THE WORLD PREMIERE PRODUCTION)

Cast of Characters

Stan Lee
Jack Kirby
Roz Kirby
Martin Goodman
Joan Lee
The Observer
Carmine Infantino
Flo Steinberg
Greer Grant
Joe Simon
Private Dugan
Corporal Pinkerton
Jack Liebowitz
Jack Schiff
Jim Mooney
Stan Goldberg
Nat Freedland
Suzie Sutton
Menahem Golan
Jim Shooter
Robert Knight
Announcer (Voice Only)

"Comics are one of the five native American art forms, including banjo music, jazz music, musical theatre, and the mystery story as invented by Edgar Allen Poe."

— *Harlan Ellison*

"Entertainment is a sacred pursuit when done well. When done well, it raises the quality of human life."

— *Michael Chabon*

FOREWORD

When I began this project, the stories that immediately grabbed me were the ones presented in parts one and two of this "Four-Color Trilogy." The inarguable injustice that the stunning egotism and arrogance of Bob Kane imposed upon Bill Finger, and the self-inflicted blow of content regulation and censorship within a vilified industry that led to the downfall of the greatest comic book publisher of the 1950s.

Where to go from there?

Well, to arguably the most important and successful partnership that ever worked within the medium of comic books.

Stan and Jack. Jack and Stan.

In the 1980s, with a wave of "relevant" and "adult" comics, there was article after article that proclaimed, "POW! ZAP! Comics Aren't Just For Kids!" Seminal works like Frank Miller's THE DARK KNIGHT RETURNS, and Alan Moore and Dave Gibbons' WATCHMEN stood on the shoulders of the work that Jack Kirby and Stan Lee launched in 1961 with THE FANTASTIC FOUR #1. Their partnership, which encompassed Kirby's fantastical and powerfully cosmic plotting and imagery, welded to Lee's sense of small-scale human problems (who before Lee ever even pondered how a superhero team might pay for residence in a midtown Manhattan skyscraper?) first opened the door to the psychological and sexual complications those like Miller and Moore dived headfirst into.

Of course, as with any partnership, the question of ego would eventually raise its head. The "Marvel Method" pioneered by Lee and Kirby was, in my humble opinion, the source of their greatness as well as eventual conflict and dissolution. Creating a true synergy of both men's talents, that also left the question of who, exactly, did what, and who the definitive "creator" was.

In the world of comic book fandom, this is the question that can inspire so much inflamed rhetoric and outright anger. It's the eternal debate, the unanswerable question that draws lines in the sand for lovers of graphic storytelling. Although, there are more than a few fans who will, with absolute certainty, tell you they have that answer.

This play you have purchased (Thank you!) is my own attempt to articulate my own relationship with, and feelings about, these two geniuses, and their magnificent works (Steve Ditko's as well).

As always, I will say upfront, THE HOUSE OF IDEAS is a work of fiction. I do not claim it is a documentary. I have altered timelines and adjusted facts to make the action and drama as effective as possible. If you are interested in Stan and Jack's lives and work, there are multiple books and documentaries available, please seek them out.

Notes

This story is loosely based on actual events and people. In certain case incidents, characters and timelines have been changed for dramatic purposes. Certain characters may be composites, or entirely fictitious.

"Marvel Comics," and associated titles are copyright and trademark of the Walt Disney Company. They are used in a narrative, historical context, and no ownership is implied.

"The New Gods," "The Fourth World," and associated titles are copyright and trademark of DC Comics. They are used in a narrative, historical context, and no ownership is implied.

A note on projections: These should be dynamic, brief, and not intrude into the scenes. Dialogue should be continuous.

The House of Ideas

ACT I

SCENE ONE

(Projected: An image of the grandeur of deep space)

(A large man in a red toga lined with comic book images is silhouetted against the image, this is our OBSERVER)

(Projected: A very rapid series of Marvel comic panels, or portions thereof as the OBSERVER speaks. Should be too quick for anything more than an impression)

OBSERVER
As fabled Atlantis rose and fell, grand Xanadu Kublai Khan decreed, and El Dorado lost to the mists of fantasy, I have observed these realms. Since time out of mind, these eyes have witnessed the path of imagination. I know all that is, most of what has been, and much of what will be.

(Projected: More cosmic majesty)

OBSERVER
Having a trivia night? Call me.

(Lights shift. The OBSERVER is fully illuminated)

OBSERVER
I am sustained by the well of inspiration. I have seen the fabulous trickery of Houdini, the heady, swirling musical journeys of Bird Parker...And the imaginings that enliven my heart, nourish my soul like no other.

(He produces a Marvel comic book. He opens it and inhales the aroma of the paper and ink)

OBSERVER
Joyously read into tatters, or slabbed safely under plastic, by...fans...like me.

(Projected: NEW YORK — 1941)

OBSERVER
A sordid enterprise born of a glorious marriage of ink and pulp paper. An art form of exciting story and explosive art that would take its first steps into maturity through a partnership that was steeped in anger and resentment before it ever started...

(Projected: Image of New York City in 1941)

(Lights fade on The OBSERVER. Lights up on four men in an office, JOE SIMON and Jacob Kurtzberg, better known by his pen name, JACK KIRBY face off with MARTIN GOODMAN, Publisher of Timely Comics. Another man sits behind GOODMAN, attempting to remain unnoticed, Stanley Lieber, who will become known as STAN LEE)

GOODMAN
You're supposed to bring ME comics, Simon.

JACK
Goodman, are you callin' us slackers?

GOODMAN
I expect you to work for ME.

(Projected: The Timely Comics logo)

SIMON
Kirby and I give you the services we contracted for. Captain America each month, like clockwork.

JACK
I ain't no welsher, you get that? I didn't take insults back in the neighborhood, and I ain't gonna do it now. I do my work, Joe does his, and sell like gangbusters! Hell, even your nephew back there...

GOODMAN
Cousin, actually.

JACK
Whatever! He didn't earn his job, but he knows to do what we tell him.

GOODMAN
I hear tell you boys have been moonlighting. That's a violation of your deal.

SIMON
The deal that gives us twenty-five percent of Captain America?

JACK
I don't see that in my checks! How's that for a valuation?

(SIMON places a hand on JACK's arm, quieting him)

GOODMAN
I think you're over-estimating the profit on that book.

SIMON
You're laying every last bit of the office expenses, all of this, against our comic!

GOODMAN
I keep clean books, Joe. If Liebowitz over at DC gets

first crack of your work, I don't see that Timely Comics needs your services.

JACK
(To STAN) You ratted us out, didn't ya kid? Followed us around like a puppy, and then ran back to Uncle Marty.

SIMON
Let it go, Jack.

GOODMAN
You did this to yourself.

SIMON
We all make deals, Goodman. Remember that when the sales come in.

(JACK and SIMON step out, lights shift to isolate them. Lights down on GOODMAN and STAN)

JACK
He screwed us, Joe!!

SIMON
It's business, don't take it personally.

JACK
I swear, I ever see that Stanley Lieber kid again, I'm gonna kill him.

SIMON
Anybody could've told Goodman we were moonlighting. Ten guys knew about it.

JACK
No, no way. That kid followed us over there, spying for Goodman.

SIMON
Jack, calm down. Bridges burn. I'm not always going to be around to have your back.

(Lights shift back to STAN and GOODMAN. JACK and SIMON exit)

GOODMAN
They're gone, Stanley. You can stop hiding back there.

STAN
I wasn't hiding, Mister Goodman.

GOODMAN
Of course not...Well, Joe Simon, my editor, just walked out. I guess it's on you now.

STAN
What was that Mister Goodman?

GOODMAN
You're in charge.

(GOODMAN starts to exit, then stops)

GOODMAN
Make more than you spend.

(GOODMAN exits. STAN is alone as the lights shift)

Scene Two

(Projected: FRANCE — 1944)

OBSERVER
The fantasy of four-color violence cannot hold against the brutal truth of war. Men in their prime answered a nation's call. Some would find glory and renown, others fear and failure, but all were left, physically and mentally, changed forever.

(Lights up on JACK. He is dressed in an infantry uniform, dirty and battered from battle)

(Projected: An image of WWII US Troops)

(Another GI, PRIVATE DUGAN, wanders in and plops down)

DUGAN
Hell of a day.

JACK
Is it like this all the time?

DUGAN
Usually the weather is worse. Be thankful you're not one of those poor bastards on the Russian front.

JACK
That bad?

DUGAN
That's the word. It's not like they tell us anything.

JACK
I hear that. Seems like just last week I was goin' to work, then wham! On a troop transport.

DUGAN
Yeah, that Hitler's damn inconsiderate.

(They share a laugh)

JACK
Name's Kurtzberg, but they call me Kirby.

DUGAN
Dugan. You from New York? Sounds like it.

JACK
The Big Apple's number-one son, lower east side.

DUGAN
(Bad French accent) "Ohh, Big Apple, passe le fromage et le champagne."

JACK
You'll offend the locals talkin' that way.

DUGAN
The Frogs are offended by anything they can't surrender to. *(Pulls out a flask)* You want a snort?

JACK
Nah. I got my own.

DUGAN
Hang on to that. Worth more than gold. That and smokes.

(DUGAN pulls CAPTAIN AMERICA COMICS #40

from his rucksack. JACK gazes at his fellow soldier)

(Projected: cover of CAPTAIN AMERICA COMICS #40)

JACK
Ya like that Captain America?

DUGAN
Better'n that fish guy with the pointed ears. The Sub-ma-REEN-er, or whatever.

JACK
Sub-MARE-in-er. Prince Namor.

DUGAN
What are you, a smartass? They give 'em to us.

JACK
You might be interested to know...

DUGAN
I don't need to know anything from you, new boy! Come back when the Ratzis have taken a few more shots at you.

JACK
Captain America. That's my guy. Me and Joe Simon.

DUGAN
Yeah, right. Gimme a break.

JACK
I'll show you...

(JACK opens his rucksack and pulls out a sketchpad. He holds it up to DUGAN)

JACK
See?

DUGAN
Aw, hell, Kirby, I could do that!

JACK
Sure ya could, wiseass.

(JACK stuffs his sketches away. Lights dim to a spotlight on JACK)

JACK
Dear Roz: I have landed on another planet. The GIs remind me that war is real, and that the Nazis who started this horror are not comic book characters. But this war...I will never forget what I have seen, the weak suffering under this evil. All I want is to get to Berlin, kill Hitler, and return home to you. I'll try to write you every day.

(Lights shift back)

DUGAN
Wait...Is that for real?

JACK
I ain't no liar.

DUGAN
So you're rich, then?

(Beat. The lights shift)

Scene Three

(Projected: Image of Fort Monmouth)

(Lights shift and we find STAN sneaking into the base mailroom. He searches the office for the key to the mailboxes, occasionally making indistinct comments to himself on his progress)

(Projected: FORT MONMOUTH, NEW JERSEY — 1945)

(Lights shift as STAN is caught in a flashlight beam)

PINKERTON *(Off stage)*
Face front, Soldier!!

(The flashlight cuts out and the overhead lights come on and a MP, CORPORAL PINKERTON, is holding his gun on STAN)

PINKERTON
Hands up!

STAN
Well, hey there!…Now, I bet you're asking yourself what I'm doing in here.

PINKERTON
Put your hands up!!

(STAN does so. PINKERTON starts to reach for his radio)

STAN
Hold on, hold on! Can't ya cut a guy a break? I'm one of the playwrights.

(Beat)

PINKERTON
Thank you for your service. Let's go.

STAN
Couldn't ya cut a fellow GI a break? I got a deadline, here. Assignment right in that box.

PINKERTON
Sounds like a problem for you and your CO.

STAN
Well, y'know, it's not really for the Army.

PINKERTON
Keeping things safe stateside, huh?

(STAN checks PINKERTON's uniform for his name)

STAN
Hey, Corporal...Pinkerton...say, Do they call you "Pinky?"

PINKERTON
Not if they want to keep their teeth.

STAN
Nobody tells their CO everything, do they?

(STAN smiles. PINKERTON doesn't)

STAN
Do ya mind if I put my hands down?

(PINKERTON lowers his gun)

STAN
So…can you help a guy out? Open the mailroom?

PINKERTON
What the hell is this job?

(Lights shift to a spot on STAN. PINKERTON freezes)

STAN
I always dreamed of becoming a household name. A bon vivant of style and grace! A wordsmith! To be uttered in the same breath as Shakespeare! Tolstoy! Twain! Synonymous with class, skill, and talent.

(Lights shift back)

STAN
(Sighs) I write comic books.

PINKERTON
Are you kidding?

STAN
'Fraid not.

(PINKERTON pulls a folded up copy of WHIZ COMICS #63 featuring Captain Marvel from his pocket)

(Projected: The Cover of WHIZ COMICS #63)

PINKERTON
Never miss me a Captain Marvel. Shazam! You write this?

(STAN looks at the book)

STAN
Y'know, that's a different publisher.

PINKERTON
Huh. Which one is yours?

STAN
Well, I tell ya...real exciting! Action packed, my friend!
Captain America, the sentinel of liberty!

(STAN does a superhero pose. Beat)

PINKERTON
Yeah...That one's terrible...You know the guy who does
these?

(The lights shift)

Scene Four

(The OBSERVER appears)

(Projected: NEW YORK, NY — 1958)

OBSERVER
The Nazis defeated, Freedom and prosperity bloomed stateside. Fighting men returned to new homes, new opportunities, and new pressures to support their growing young families...

(Projected: The 1950s DC Comics logo)

OBSERVER
...But deception and betrayal breed in peacetime, as well.

(Lights shift to the DC Comics offices. JACK walks onstage carrying his portfolio, a light rises and reveals JACK SCHIFF, an editor)

SCHIFF
Kirby! Come in here, we need to talk.

JACK
What do you need Schiff?

SCHIFF
You were supposed to wet my beak.

JACK
"Wet your beak?" What? Did ya join the mob?

SCHIFF
We had an agreement.

JACK
Are you jokin'? We paid you!

SCHIFF
It's money. It's never funny. You made a first installment.
We said four percent.

JACK
Of everything? That's insane! D'ya think I'm a dope?

(SCHIFF smiles and shrugs)

SCHIFF
Not many games left in town, Kirby. What with you
having such a nice little house out in Long Island, three
beautiful kids...and another on the way...It'd be a real
shame if DC no longer needed your services. Yeah, that
would be a real damn shame.

JACK
Ya ain't nothin' but a crook. This is a scam!

SCHIFF
The word is "business," Kirby.

*(JACK gathers his portfolio, and exits. As he walks across
the stage, lights shift to the Kirby home, ROZ KIRBY,
Jack's wife bustles about. She is pregnant. There is a radio
playing and she sways and sings to Frank Sinatra's
"All the Way." As JACK enters the scene, she turns off the
radio and kisses him)*

ROZ
There's my man! How was the train?

JACK
Be faster if you let me drive.

ROZ
You don't drive. I drive. You don't make enough to pay for a fourth wrecked car, Kirby.

(JACK sits and slumps)

ROZ
What's the matter?

(She wedges herself into his lap. JACK grunts)

ROZ
Oh, stop that! My Kirby can lift a car if he needs to!

JACK
You must be cookin' a Buick in there, then.

(She smacks him playfully)

ROZ
Keep it up mister smart guy, and I'll send you to bed with no supper.

JACK
It's physically impossible for Roz Kirby, my ever-lovin' wife, to not force-feed every man, woman or child in sight. I bet every last one of Neal's friends left here with a sandwich AND a piece of cake! Am I right?

ROZ
That's none of your business!

JACK
(Sighs) That damn word.

ROZ
What word?

JACK
"Business."

ROZ
What happened?

JACK
That…

(JACK scans the area)

JACK
Kids around?

ROZ
Outside playing.

JACK
That GODDAMNED Jack Schiff wanted a kickback! It was like being worked over by the gangs back in the neighborhood.

ROZ
You're too good for those rats. I hope you told him what's what.

JACK
I told him he could take his low-rent books and shove 'em!

ROZ
That's my fella.

(They kiss. ROZ gets up and returns to her chores)

JACK
I don't know where I'm gonna go. Schiff's gonna blackball me at DC. The whole damn industry is on it's last legs, thanks to that Wertham creep. The guys holdin' the strings are a buncha' crooks. In the neighborhood, If some jerk was tryin' ta put one over on ya, ya'd paste

him in the kisser, and they'd back off...I sure wish Joe was still around.

ROZ
Call him.

JACK
Ah, hell, Roz. Joe Simon's out of the business, Simon and Kirby is long over...I'm a grown man, I got three kids and you to take care of. Ought to be able to handle this.

ROZ
We can take care of ourselves. I'll give Schiff a sock in the jaw for ya.

JACK
Hell, I outta turn you loose on that scumbag. All the scraps I had back in the neighborhood, all those bums. Ain't nobody who scared me, not one. Except you.

ROZ
Didn't seem so scared when you asked me up to your bedroom to see your etchings...

JACK
Jeeze, Roz...we were kids!

ROZ
Here I thought you were making a pass, and you pull out a bunch of drawings!

JACK
Our parents were right there!

ROZ
Details, Kirby. Details.

(She kisses him. JACK is quiet)

ROZ
What are you chewin' on?

JACK
I heard Goodman might need guys.

ROZ
Kirby, you can't. They welched on you and Joe! You want to work for Stanley Lieber?

JACK
Can't be worse than Jack Schiff.

ROZ
Bunch of finks. You can smell 'em, Kirby, you always could.

JACK
Then why can't I get a decent deal without Joe?

ROZ
You will.

JACK
Not if we all starve to death first. I'm goin' down to the dungeon to work.

ROZ
Remember to eat!

JACK
Like you wouldn't tie a feed bag to my face!

(JACK exits, and the lights fade)

Scene Five

(Projected: LONG ISLAND, NY)

(Lights shift to a cocktail party at GOODMAN's home. Charlie Parker's "Everything Happens to Me" plays softly. STAN and his wife, JOAN LEE, stand holding martinis and laughing in her English accent with GOODMAN)

(Projected: Photo of a Long Island Estate)

JOAN
Oh Martin! You are such a CARD!

(They all laugh)

JOAN
Is Jean going to join us?

GOODMAN
She'll be out presently. Something to do with the staff in the kitchen.

JOAN
Good help is hard to find, Martin. Don't we know that, Stan?

STAN
What do you mean? We don't have...

(JOAN elbows him)

STAN
YES! So right, Joanie! Our last pool party was almost a disaster. TERRIBLE help!

GOODMAN
I'm sorry Jean and I weren't able to make it.

JOAN
Next time, Martin! We always have a martini ready for you.

GOODMAN
Maybe you'd like to join her in the kitchen.

JOAN
Oh, I don't think so.

(She turns away from GOODMAN)

STAN
Y'know, Martin, I have some exciting ideas for expanding the magazine line...

JOAN
Yes! Stan was regaling me with the idea. Celebrity photos, witty commentary. What were you going to call it Stan?

STAN
Celebrity!

GOODMAN
Pardon me, Stanley. I see someone important.

(GOODMAN exits)

STAN
Another time, Martin!

JOAN
Oh, Stan...Jean's new couch is just darling! That's a Carl Hansen, I just know it. I should look into getting one.

STAN
Maybe wait until we've paid off the sideboard?

JOAN
The Danish school just speaks to me.

STAN
Danish! It's imported?

JOAN
Of course it is! Who buys American? No one with style.

(GREER GRANT enters, carrying a notebook)

GREER
Excuse me, are you friends of the Goodmans?

JOAN
Relatives, darling.

GREER
Oh really?

JOAN
My husband is Martin's nephew.

STAN
Cousin, actually.

JOAN
Stanley and I live just down the block.

GREER
Isn't that just delicious!

JOAN
I like to think so.

GREER
Well, I'll have to cover your next party.

JOAN
Cover?

GREER
Oh, I do the social page for The South Shore Record.
Greer Grant.

JOAN
The South Shore Record! Stan, isn't that just wonderful!?

STAN
Sure is. My name is Stanley Lieber, by the way. This is
my wife Joanie.

GREER
Absolutely charmed! You're here in the neighborhood?

JOAN
Right down the street. You MUST come by, I have some
lovely pieces I found at a little boutique in Greenwich…
the city? I really think they might be Gio Ponti. Maybe
you can give me your opinion?

GREER
I would absolutely LOVE to! May I call you Joan?

JOAN
OF COURSE!

GREER
What do you do, Stan? Oh, may I call you Stan?

STAN
Anything but "hey Bozo!" and to tell you the truth, that's
probably OK by me, too! I work for Martin's company.

GREER
Magazine Management?

STAN
That's absolutely right. Say, you ARE a reporter, aren't you!

(They all laugh)

JOAN
She's got a notebook! Be careful what you say, Stan.

GREER
The magazine business is soooo very interesting.

STAN
I happen to be a writer. Along with some editing and art direction.

GREER
How exciting! What do you work on?

STAN
...You probably haven't heard of it, it's children's publications.

JOAN
It's just such a niche market, even with our daughter, J.C? I've never heard of half these magazines Stan talks about.

GREER
My nephews are voracious readers. I'm sure they read EVERY, SINGLE children's magazine.

(JOAN looks at STAN)

STAN
They're...illustrated stories.

GREER
Like what?

STAN
It's actually comic books, Greer. I run Martin's line of comic books.

(Beat)

GREER
Well, it was...lovely to meet you both. Unfortunately, I simply must rush back to the office and file this story.

JOAN
Well I very much hope you'll be able to stop by and help authenticate my Gio Ponti.

GREER
Honestly, Mrs. Lieber, I'm quite sure it wouldn't be genuine.

(GREER exits. STAN picks at a spot on his tie, and JOAN sips her martini. Lights shift)

Scene Six

(Lights shift. The OBSERVER appears)

(Projected: Image of Joe Maneely)

OBSERVER

Look upon the visage of one Joe Maneely. In more than one other world or alternate timeline, Joe Maneely is the artist who would join Stan Lee in this creative campaign. For a moment in time, it was not inevitable that the pencil of Jack Kirby would provide the yin to the yang of Stan Lee's desires.

(Projected: A shadow puppet style animation where Maneely falls from a subway train)

OBSERVER

A twist of poor luck, one drink too many, slipped attention in a crucial moment, and a young life of creative promise reduced to a footnote.

(Projected: a 1958 Empire State Building Observatory advertisement)

(Lights shift to STAN, alone in the offices of the now Atlas comics. He sits at his tiny desk in this tiny office. A bottle of whiskey and a shot glass on his desk)

(Projected: ATLAS COMICS OFFICES, THE EMPIRE STATE BUILDING)

(STAN raises a drink)

STAN
To Joe Maneely! Always good for a laugh, could draw anything. The BEST partner a guy could ask for. If only we could've gotten a newspaper strip to stick.

(Projected: Examples of the "Willie Lumpkin" and "Mrs. Lyon's Cubs" newspaper strips)

(STAN pours another drink, and wipes away a tear)

STAN
What am I going to do without you, buddy?

JACK *(Off stage)*
Stanley?

OBSERVER
Yet, in every tragedy, an opportunity...

(The OBSERVER exits)

STAN
Who's there?!

(JACK enters)

STAN
Jack?

(STAN jumps up and grasps his hand, then pulls the smaller man in for a hug)

STAN
Kirby? It's great to see you! Everybody else is already gone.

JACK
What the hell? You been crying?

STAN
You're not here for Joe?

JACK
You better start makin' some sort of sense quick, Stanley.

STAN
Joe Maneely...he was out with some of the guys last night and...I guess he should've stopped before that last drink...

(STAN starts to tear up again)

JACK
Take it easy, Stanley. Here, siddown.

(JACK angles STAN into a chair)

STAN
He slipped off the train platform.

JACK
Holy crap, he was only a kid. Couldn't have been more than thirty.

STAN
Thirty-two, I think. Poor Betty Jean, and those three beautiful little girls. He was my go-to guy, Jack, my right hand.

JACK
Boy, that's a kick in the teeth. I hope Goodman's taking care of them. I don't know what Roz would do if I went down.

STAN
I don't know what I'm gonna do. Goodman finally let

us do new work. Atlas was almost back on track, Joe was
the backbone.

JACK
Atlas?

(Projected: The Atlas Comics logo)

STAN
Martin changes the name of the company like he changes
his shirt. I think it keeps the taxman confused.

JACK
Of course it does.

STAN
It seemed so much more fun before the war. Those
were the days, huh? You, Joe Simon, and I cranking out
Captain America.

JACK
You got us coffee.

STAN
I just never understood why you and Joe ran off. We had
a good thing going!

JACK
Are you kiddin'? You followed us over to the hotel, and
then ran back to Goodman. Ya squealed on us, Stanley!

STAN
Jack, I swear...

JACK
I need ya to shut yer yap, OK? This is hard enough.

(Beat)

JACK
I need work.

STAN
I thought you were at DC with Jack Schiff?

JACK
What I'm with is a wife, three kids and a mortgage. Yer a rat, but not a crook.

STAN
Jack...

JACK
Look, Stanley, I still got some pride. I need work, but I ain't gonna beg.

(*JACK begins to exit*)

STAN
Hold on, hold on, Jack!! Why the heck didn't you call me? Of course you have a place here! All that Wertham nonsense has us doing a lot of silly monster books.

JACK
Monsters?

STAN
Space creatures, atomic mutants, whatever! Just like the movies. Goodman never saw a bandwagon he couldn't run the wheels off. C'mon, sit down! I've got something for you. A title I cooked up for Journey into Mystery; "Creatures in the Volcano!!" How's that sound?

JACK
What's it about?

STAN
Creatures...in a volcano.

(*Projected: The first page of "Creatures in the Volcano!" from* JOURNEY INTO MYSTERY *#51*)

(*Lights shift*)

Scene Seven

(Projected: Photo of the Inwood Country Club)

(MARTIN GOODMAN and JACK LIEBOWITZ, publisher of DC comics, are playing golf. GOODMAN takes a swing. LIEBOWITZ watches the shot fly down the fairway)

(Projected: INWOOD COUNTRY CLUB - 1960)

LIEBOWITZ
Not bad, Martin.

GOODMAN
Thank you.

LIEBOWITZ
Uh oh! Looks like you hooked it right into the rough. Story of your life, huh?

(LIEBOWTIZ peers down the fairway)

LIEBOWITZ
How many monthly books are you down to, now?

GOODMAN
You know exactly how many, Liebowitz. What you allow us to. Eight.

LIEBOWITZ
(Chuckles) Eight books…You made the deal, Goodman. Your distributor goes belly up. We at DC comics were happy to lend a hand to…what is it this week? Atlas Comics?

GOODMAN
You pushed your advantage, Jack

LIEBOWITZ
I think that's called "business," Martin.

(LIEBOWITZ sets up his shot)

GOODMAN
I see you're doing superheroes again.

LIEBOWITZ
The Flash, then Green Lantern, the whole bit, but that was only the appetizer.

GOODMAN
You don't say.

LIEBOWITZ
Team books, Goodman. Bring 'em all together. Kids know; why drop a dime for one superhero, when you can get five?

(LIEBOWITZ swings, and slices even worse than GOODMAN)

GOODMAN
Huh. You don't say.

(Lights shift, revealing STAN back in the Atlas offices. STAN holds a piece of paper, upon which is scrawled in

block letters, "PULITZER PRIZE")

STAN
To think that my little ol' novel, my VERY FIRST! Would be proclaimed the greatest of the great American novels! And, at such a tender young age, the jury would see fit to place this award in my hands, and the name Stanley Martin Lieber into the pantheon of greats like Cather, Sinclair Lewis, Steinbeck! I just want to thank everyone who...

(GOODMAN enters, still dressed for golf)

GOODMAN
Stanley? Who are you talking to?

(STAN quickly hides his prop)

STAN
Uh, no one, Martin.

GOODMAN
Mister Goodman, Stanley. We're at work.

STAN
Won't happen again, Mister Goodman.

GOODMAN
I don't need people talking about my wife's looney cousin yabbering to himself. You're my editor, Stanley. Act like it. It wouldn't be hard to find someone else.

STAN
So you keep telling me.

GOODMAN
What was that?

STAN
Nothing! Mar...Mister Goodman.

(Beat)

GOODMAN
You're spending a lot of my money.

STAN
These men have families. Jack Kirby just had another little girl, and when he draws a mag, it sells!

GOODMAN
No one likes putting men on the street, especially with kids. Chip is the joy of my life...But this is about waste. A whole file full of unpublished work we didn't need.

STAN
Jack's firing on all cylinders!...A tree monster from space called "Groot!"

GOODMAN
What's a Groot?

STAN
Monsters, like you asked for. Let me show you the art...

(STAN holds up TALES TO ASTONISH #13, featuring the debut of Groot! The Monster from Planet X!)

(Projected: the cover of TALES TO ASTONISH #13)

GOODMAN
A tree?

STAN
Well, it's not really...I know it's all kind of silly, but I think we found a nice little angle.

GOODMAN
Listen to me, Stanley. No more monsters.

STAN
No more monsters?

GOODMAN
No. More. Monsters. The fad's over, Stan. You know what DC's biggest book is?

STAN
Well, I saw they were bringing back...

GOODMAN
They just got the numbers on this, and it's huge.

(GOODMAN *pulls out a roughly folded copy of THE BRAVE AND THE BOLD # 28, with a cover featuring the Justice League of America*)

(*Projected: The cover of THE BRAVE AND BOLD #28*)

STAN
Superheroes?

GOODMAN
Liebowitz has me over a barrel. Crowing about sales, like he owns the whole newsstand.

STAN
DC IS carrying us for distribution.

GOODMAN
I had to keep our heads above water, but I want to beat him at his own game.

STAN
Won't be easy when we can only ship eight books a month.

GOODMAN
I want superheroes like DC, Stanley. Yesterday, if not sooner. You're reasonably competent, family, and my editor. So do what I tell you.

STAN
Bring back the Sub-Mariner? Captain Ameri—

GOODMAN
Don't even say it! I don't want Joe Simon's grief.

STAN
It was a popular book.

GOODMAN
Kirby'll do what he's told, he needs the money.

STAN
Jack IS the best we have.

GOODMAN
You're the editor, you're in charge.

(*GOODMAN starts to exit, stops short*)

GOODMAN
Monsters ARE selling...Do Something like that starfish thing.

(*GOODMAN exits. Lights shift*)

SCENE EIGHT

(Lights shift to the Kirby home. The "dungeon," where JACK toils, shirtless, over his drafting table in a straight-backed chair. Judy Garland's "I'm Always Chasing Rainbows" is playing softly. ROZ enters, exhausted)

JACK
Lisa finally sleeping?

ROZ
Yes. Thank God. I swear, Kirby, no more babies.

JACK
Where's the fun in that?

ROZ
Then you can handle the labor.

JACK
I think you'd have to take that request to a higher authority.

ROZ
You should come to bed.

JACK
Gotta finish this, then start on the next batch.

ROZ
What's this one about?

JACK
(Sighs) Same as the last one. Monstro, or Sporr, or whatever. It's all blending together. Tentacles, teeth, fins, rinse and repeat. I tell ya, I miss the heroes. Something to look up to, not just one atomic disaster after another. The Challengers of the Unknown fought these kinds of monsters. Something to aspire to.

(Projected: Kirby's cover for TALES OF SUSPENSE #8, featuring Monstro)

ROZ
Maybe you should talk to Stanley.

JACK
Ah, Roz. Stanley Lieber is so far up Martin Goodman, it ain't just his nose that's brown.

ROZ
I hope you don't talk that way in front of the kids.

JACK
(Chuckles) Neal's almost thirteen, Roz. I think he understands the concept of a brown-nose.

ROZ
I don't want him to hear about it from you!

JACK
Okay, Okay! I don't want to get on your bad side.

ROZ
You are a wise man, Kirby.

JACK
Then why ain't I rich?

(Lights shift to the Lee residence. STAN is sitting at his typewriter. Music shifts to Miles Davis' "Freddie Freeloader." JOAN saunters in with a martini)

JOAN
JC is finally asleep.

STAN
Hallelujah.

JOAN
That child will be the death of me.

STAN
Her mother's daughter.

JOAN
Bite your tongue. Just for that, Mister Stanley Lieber, you owe me a dance.

(She pulls him away from the typewriter)

STAN
Joan, I really need to work.

(They begin to dance around the room)

JOAN
I remember a young man who promised to dance with me forever.

STAN
Sounds like a pretty desperate kid.

JOAN
Oh, you wouldn't believe it. Just a pain in the ass!

(They kiss. JOAN indicates the typewriter as the dance continues)

JOAN

Are you finally starting your novel? Is it about a young man with an undying love for an English war bride, convincing her to leave her decent but oh-so-boring husband for a quickie divorce in Reno?

STAN

Ohhh, she should be a hat model!

JOAN

Ooooooh! How original!

STAN

Maybe she should write him a letter calling him by the wrong name, so he has to fly to Nevada in a panic to make sure she hasn't taken up with a fly-by-night gambler.

JOAN

Oh, poo! Dear John, Dear Stan? Who can keep track of these things?

(STAN dips her)

STAN

I can when I'm paying for the hat model to go to Reno.

(He kisses her)

JOAN

Hmm, I love a man who takes charge.

(The dance ends)

STAN

My dear, if I was in charge, I wouldn't feel like I'm going backward. Superheroes again. This week, anyway.

JOAN

Why don't you just quit?

STAN
I'd just like to write something BETTER.

JOAN
What do you want to write?

STAN
Even for teenagers would feel like a victory.

JOAN
Martin wants these superheroes, fine! Write them your way. What's the worst that could happen? It fails? He hates it? THEN you quit.

STAN
How would I pay for your faux Gio Ponti, then?

JOAN
It's better than being afraid. *(Turns to exit)* And we don't know it's faux!

(JOAN exits. Lights shift)

Scene Nine

(STAN and JACK are meeting in Stan's office)

STAN
Goodman wants superheroes, but I want to do something different, Jackson.

JACK
I want to pay my mortgage. *(Beat)* Different? This sounds a hell of a lot like that book I did for DC...

(Projected: CHALLENGERS OF THE UNKNOWN #8)

STAN
Who remembers Challengers of the Unknown, Jack?

JACK
I do....But you're the editor.

STAN
And Martin's the publisher...I think this can work! It's about HOW we do it! Survivors of an experimental rocket crash, a big genius, a tough guy pilot, a cocky kid...

JACK
And a girl.

STAN
Well, c'mon, we need a girl. We're trying to reach a wider audience here.

JACK
I did romance books, Stanley...This plot? Another monster story, freaks hiding out under an island. You think girls wanna read that?

STAN
The key is superheroes that seem like your neighbors!

JACK
We've got an ape with a rocky hide, a rubber guy, an invisible socialite and a smartass kid who bursts into flame...who the hell lives in your neighborhood?

STAN
They argue! They bicker! They have money problems!

JACK
I know my kids think the Wall Street Journal is the bees knees.

STAN
Just a little, tiny, bit more real. Doesn't what I'm taking about excite you at all, Jackson?

JACK
It's easy for you, Stanley. Everybody knows you're one foot out the door. I need this job!

STAN
C'mon, Jack! That's not true!

JACK
The hell it ain't! Not two weeks ago word was you were

gonna quit. I'm not gonna be the last one without a seat when the music stops, and you're out the door.

STAN
Jack, we can sell this thing! Take your astonishing art, your incomparable imagination, and put people we recognize in it. People who can't pay the bills, who kvetch and suffer. Look at poor Ben! Trapped inside an ugly, monstrous body.

JACK
I gotta admit, I like that Ben Grimm.

STAN
The ever-lovin' blue-eyed Thing!

JACK
(Chuckles) Reminds me of the neighborhood.

STAN
Jack, look…Just this once, I want to try something a little better. Just a little bit of realism, pathos and humanity. I know they're comic books, but…I just think that we, you and I, Jackson, WE can make them better.

(Beat)

JACK
Stanley, you really want to blow the doors off?

STAN
Would I lie to you?

JACK
Then we gotta do better than a reheated monster story. I got some designs, characters…

STAN
Now you're cookin' Jackson!!

JACK

We can take this thing places no one's ever dreamed of. Mythology, epic stuff. Monsters? How about Gods?

STAN

Jack, I wanna hear all about it. I do! We get this first issue out...

JACK

You say that now. We're gonna break our backs for a tryout book that only exists because Goodman wants to show up Liebowitz. You know as well as I do that he might see a western next week and decide to chuck all this for more Rawhide Kid.

STAN

I think we can do something so much better, so much more exciting and pulse-pounding than another Martin Goodman bandwagon book. He wants this... *(Holds up THE BRAVE AND THE BOLD #28)* We Give it to him, and sneak in a whole new way of doing comics! I believe in you Jack. The best comic book artist in the world. The King of Comics!! We're going to show guys like Jack Schiff...

JACK

Don't even MENTION Jack Schiff to me!!

STAN

You and I...Stan the Man and King Kirby!

JACK

Don't break your arm with that "Stan the Man" stuff. *(Beat)* I'm gonna trust you, Stanley.

(STAN looks at THE BRAVE AND THE BOLD cover again)

STAN

But, y'know, Jack....we don't wanna give Martin a chance

to shut us down.

(Projected: THE BRAVE AND BOLD #28)

STAN
Make the cover match this as much as you can. I can tweak the cover copy; "Together for the first time in one mighty magazine!!" That way they sound like established characters.

JACK
You want a giant starfish, too?

(Projected: The cover of THE FANTASTIC FOUR #1 joins the Justice League cover. They remain for a moment, then THE BRAVE AND BOLD #28 fades, leaving only THE FANTASTIC FOUR #1)

(Lights shift)

Scene Ten

(The OBSERVER steps in front of the cover image)

OBSERVER
Stan and Jack. Jack and Stan. Would Joe Maneely's artwork have erupted off the page to fuel the life-long fantasies of a generation of comic book readers? Possibly? But the super-powered myths that have brought me before you could only come from these two men. Driven by ambition and chafing from limitations, fueled by a confidence of experience. A partnership that, no matter how much they might wish otherwise in the years to come, would define the rest of their lives. Page by page, panel by panel…

(Projected: NOVEMBER 1961)

OBSERVER
…a marvelous new age was unleashed upon yearning minds!

(A light rises on JACK, hunched over his drawing table, shirtless in his straight-backed chair)

JACK
Roz! I need another box of pencils!

ROZ *(Off stage)*
Hold your horses, Kirby!

(The light shifts to reveal STAN behind a desk. MARTIN GOODMAN enters. JACK and STAN should both remain visible throughout the scene, working in their own spaces)

GOODMAN
Stanley! I see you got our Justice League off the ground.

STAN
The Fantastic Four, Mister Goodman.

GOODMAN
I suppose...It's a little odd.

STAN
We're trying something new, Mister Goodman.

GOODMAN
"Mister Fantastic?" That's a little pedestrian, don't you think? And no costumes to go with the ridiculous codenames?

(STAN picks up a letter)

GOODMAN
Stanley, did you hear me?

STAN
Just reading fan mail, Mister Goodman!

GOODMAN
Fan mail? Can't argue with that.

(FLO STEINBERG enters)

STAN
Fabulous Flo Steinberg! Bringing me more fan mail?

FLO
What fan mail?

STAN
You're not helping, Flo.

(GOODMAN gives STAN a look and exits)

FLO
Did I do something wrong?

STAN
No, no Flo. I've just got to call in the nuclear option.

(FLO exits. STAN picks up a phone. Lights up on JIM MOONEY)

MOONEY
Jim Mooney. Shoot, it's your nickel.

STAN
Jim! Stan Lee here, how ya been?

MOONEY
Stan! Buddy! Good to hear from you. I see you and Kirby's new book. You need some costumes on these guys.

STAN
What is it with all you people and costumes?

MOONEY
If you're calling, you need something. Cough it up.

STAN
I need fan mail. How ya feel about seeing your name in print?

MOONEY
The ol' fake fan letter gag? You must be desperate! Try some costumes!

(MOONEY hangs up)

STAN
Innovation is lost on these people.

(Lights shift, and MOONEY turns out to perform his 'letter')

(Projected: An image of the Fantastic Four villain Puppetmaster controlling the FF)

MOONEY
Dear Editor, how about bios of Stan Lee and Jack Kirby? You play this game like The Fantastic Four are real people, then Stan and Jack must be figments of our imagination! – Jim Mooney: Hollywood, California

(Lights shift, MOONEY exits)

STAN
Mooney of Hollywood! He's gonna think he's a big shot.

(ROZ enters with a sandwich for JACK, and watches STAN turn out and perform)

STAN
We're as real as Aunt Petunia's cookies Jimmy boy! But we have to lie low, since every time Kirby poses for a picture, he breaks the camera lens!

ROZ
No one talks about my Kirby that way!

JACK
Let it go Roz, the books are sellin'.

STAN
And Lee? He loves "I" and "me" so much we had to widen the doors for his head!

ROZ
That's for sure!

(ROZ exits)

(Projected: The cover of THE FANTASTIC FOUR #3, featuring new costumes)

STAN
But public demand can't be ignored forever. Speaking of demand, keep your eyes peeled for developments in the costume and headquarters department. Never let it be said that the demands of our readers are anything but marching orders!

(STAN drops his performance)

STAN
Some demand! One fake letter.

(Projected: April 1962)

STAN
Hey Flo!

(FLO enters)

FLO
What do you need, Stan?

(STAN produces a letter)

STAN
Read this!

(Lights shift, FLO produces a sombrero and broadly performs the letter)

(Projected: The Puppetmaster image again)

FLO
Dear Editor; aye carumba! When The Thing put on his new costume and grumbled, 'Bah! Costumes - that's kid stuff, Who needs 'em?' I nearly flipped! At last characters that are unpredictable, and unforgettable! Mucho gusto!
– Anthony Gonzalez, Mexico City, Mexico

(Lights shift)

STAN

International recognition!

FLO

When did we start distributing in Mexico?

STAN

What are you, a lawyer?

(He grabs the letter back, FLO exits)

JACK

Stanley, I want to bring back Namor. Little tip a' the hat to Bill Everett.

STAN

The Sub-Mariner?

JACK

We bring him back as a villain. Hell, he tried to trash the Big Apple back in the 40's.

(STAN turns out and addresses his readers)

STAN

I tell ya, readers, it's become obvious...unlike the letters in mags from our lesser competition, our fans, every one, write intelligently and clearly. And they know their history! So, watch out for some exciting guest stars from the days of WWII exploding into the lives of your fantastic foursome! Don't miss out! Have your dealer hold every action-packed issue...Or don't say we didn't warn you!

(Projected: May 1962)

(Projected: The cover of THE FANTASTIC FOUR #4 reviving the Sub-Mariner)

(ROZ enters)

ROZ
Kirby, are you gonna come to bed?

JACK
I can bang out another couple a' pages tonight.

ROZ
You're pushing' too hard Jack.

JACK
Roz, the iron is hot, Goodman and Stanley want more material. Lisa's asthma ain't goin' nowhere. The doctor bills ain't either.

ROZ
My hero.

JACK
Plus...Y'know, Roz...

ROZ
You're having fun?

JACK
I haven't been this excited, this free, since I split with Joe Simon.

ROZ
I can tell. You got a sparkle.

JACK
And ta think, working with that beanpole, Stanley Lieber!...He lets me run, Roz. He leaves me be to draw everything I can draw. I tell ya, I get excited every time I start a page...I mean, Stanley doesn't always get the idea, but it's on the page.

ROZ
Maybe you oughta tell him.

JACK
What? Are you kiddin'? I ain't gonna give him that satisfaction!

(Lights shift. FLO enters and hands STAN a letter. The OBSERVER appears, carrying a surfboard, with zinc oxide on his nose)

FLO
Mail, Stan.

STAN
Hey Flo! A REAL fan letter!?

OBSERVER
Dear Editor, The way you answer some of these wiseacres is wicked, dude! I've had it with these kooks making excuses for other lame-o heroes! BUT DUDE!... on the cover of FF#3 the Torch had TWO LEFT HANDS, DUDE! – Ronn Foss, Suisun, California

(Projected: The cover of THE FANTASTIC FOUR #3, featuring The Human Torch with two left hands)

(Lights shift, FLO and the OBSERVER exit)

STAN
Ah, but he DID have five fingers on each, huh Ronn?...

JACK
You sure you didn't write that one, Stanley? I don't need guff when I'm busting my ass!

STAN
(Ignoring JACK) ...You must be a regular reader, as you are a...dude with exceptional taste in comic mags! Maybe we should call the FF THE WORLD'S WICKEDEST COMIC MAGAZINE!!

(STAN comes out of performance)

STAN

(To JACK) Good stuff, huh? "The world's wickedest comic mag!"

JACK

Shakespeare must be sweatin'. You ever gonna get around to telling me what we're doing for the next issue?

(Lights shift. JOAN, carrying a home furnishings catalog, enters and speaks with STAN)

JOAN

Stan, I'm looking at these drapes...

STAN

Joanie, my love is like the eternally beating heart of Aphrodite...but I know absolutely nothing about drapes.

JOAN

You could at least look at them.

STAN

I've got six scripts on deadline!

(JOAN leans down and kisses him)

JOAN

Oh, to be Stan Lee, wrapped in the chains of success! Oh, the burden of genius!

STAN

Your advice got me into this, young lady! Martin fixed the distribution, and now eight monthly books isn't enough. Everything's selling, and I've only got two hands and one typewriter!

(Beat)

JOAN

I'll just pick the ones I like.

STAN
No more velvet!

JOAN
Stan "no opinion" Lee...

(Lights shift. JOAN exits. The OBSERVER enters, dressed as a teenager, and carrying a notepad. He moves to JACK, who is chewing a cigar, and putting on his shirt. A fog machine simulates the smoke)

OBSERVER
Mister Kirby, thank you for this interview.

JACK
No problem kid. Sorry about the smoke. Most people work for money, I work for cigars!

(They both laugh)

JACK
What was your handle again?

OBSERVER
Len Wein.

JACK
Always happy to gab with the fans, Lenny.

OBSERVER
How old are you?

JACK
Thirty-nine, but, if you ask me, I'm ageless!

(More laughter. ROZ enters)

ROZ
You boys hungry?

JACK
If ya tell her no, Lenny, she'll take it personal.

OBSERVER
I guess I better say yes then.

ROZ
Smart kid.

(ROZ exits)

OBSERVER
How long have you been drawing comics?

JACK
Thirty-nine years! *(Laughs)* That's how it feels, anyway. Drawing on my parent's wall, then BAM! Fleischer Studios, doing animation. Backgrounds and other stuff no one else wanted to do.

OBSERVER
Wow! I never would've guessed! Where did you go to art school?

JACK
The school of hard knocks, bucko!...Just kiddin' ya. One, single solitary day at the Pratt Institute, then the depression hit, and I was out sellin' newspapers!

(The lights shift. STAN turns to JACK)

STAN
Jack, Goodman likes the numbers on the FF.

JACK
Ain't nobody who don't like money...

STAN
He wants more, and I don't have enough hours in the day.

JACK
...and everybody wants more of it. Goodman knows to keep riding on a good horse.

STAN
Here's what I want to do: You and I will talk out the story, and then you draw it up however you want, pace it out visually, and then I'll do the final dialogue based on your art. It'll be fun! Like a crossword puzzle!

JACK
You want me to write the books?

STAN
Well, I wouldn't call it that. I mean, it's my words.

JACK
Look, Stanley, I know I'm just a jabroni from the neighborhood, but when you lay out the story, you're writing.

STAN
Jack, think about it however you want.

(Beat)

JACK
You're the editor.

(The lights shift back)

OBSERVER
You plot the Fantastic Four stories? Lay out the action, and Stan fills in the dialogue?

JACK
This is Stanley's editorial policy. I'm a freelancer, I do what the editor says.

(Light shift. The OBSERVER exits. STAN turns to JACK again)

STAN
Now, look, I was thinking about another monster-type hero. Kinda like The Thing, or Frankenstein.

JACK
More monsters?

STAN
It's working. Why rock the boat?

JACK
You wanna blow the kids' minds? I got just the thing. Norse Mythology. Thor, Odin, Loki, Maybe we could...

STAN
A big, hulking monster!

JACK
Or not.

STAN
Maybe a meek and mild scientist, exposed to some sort of radiation?

JACK
Like a Jekyll and Hyde thing?

STAN
Oh! That's good! Switch back and forth, totally out of his control.

JACK
Maybe make him green?

STAN
Green?

JACK
You said Frankenstein.

STAN
Jack, who wants to look at a big green monster? Let's go with gray.

JACK
You're the...

STAN
The editor!? See, we're reading each other's minds now!

(Projected: The cover of THE INCREDIBLE HULK #1)

STAN
And so our cursed hero finds a moment of respite—but only for now! Soon the Hulk will strike again—in the next pulse-pounding issue of The Incredible Hulk! Don't let your friends read it before you!

JACK
(Chuckles) I gotta admit, Stanley, ya know how to sell a book.

STAN
Hey, while I have you...we need more letters, got any ideas?

JACK
I'm not doing ALL your work for you, Stanley.

(JACK turns back to his drawing table)

STAN
Troubled is the head that wears the crown. Hey! Goldberg!

(STAN GOLDBERG enters, he's a small, slow-speaking man)

GOLDBERG
What...Do you need, Stan? I'm working...on coloring... issue...five.

STAN
You mind if I use your name on a fan letter, Stan?

GOLDBERG
Well…That sounds OK…I guess…Whatever I can do.

STAN
You're a team player, Stan!

(*Lights shift, and* GOLDBERG, *suddenly quite animated, performs the letter*)

(*Projected: The Puppetmaster image again*)

GOLDBERG
Dear Editor: Have you flipped your lids? "Heroes" with the same jealousies and fragile egos as real people!? I guess you think your readers are sharp enough to appreciate all that good writing jazz. If you want my opinion — you're darn right! – S. Goldberg, Forest Hills, New York.

(*Lights shift,* GOLDBERG *shrinks into his more natural state, and exits*)

STAN
Whew! You scared me for a minute there, S. G.! But in just a short time The Fantastic Four has become the most talked-about comic mag in the country! So, Stan the Man says go tell all your friends to stop talking about it and start buying it…

(*JACK spins around from his desk*)

JACK
So, Stanley, this new bad guy, here's my idea…the mask?

STAN
He's deformed!

JACK
Well, yeah…but…

STAN
His face horrifically scarred, like the Phantom of the Opera!

(STAN briefly "performs" the Phantom)

JACK
Nah, nah, ya gotta think psychologically. He's an egomaniac, right?

STAN
Sure.

(JACK briefly gives STAN a meaningful look)

JACK
Totally self-absorbed.

STAN
Right right right!

JACK
This "terrible deformity" is a single, tiny scar on his perfect cheek.

(Beat)

STAN
Forget it, we just won't show his face.

(Projected: June 1962)

(Projected: The cover of THE FANTASTIC FOUR #5, featuring Doctor Doom)

(Music Stinger. Lights shift)

(Projected: An image of STEVE DITKO)

STAN
Jack. I just had a discussion with Steve...

JACK
Ditko? How'd he make out on that Spider thing? I still think the Silver Spider's a better name.

STAN
Jack, I wanted a teenager. You drew him like Captain America. Ditko's stuff is weirder, more human.

JACK
But ya still wanted me to do the cover.

STAN
Jack! You're the king, you know that!

(Projected: August 1962)

(Projected: The cover of AMAZING FANTASY #15, the debut of Spider-Man. STAN performs again)

STAN
As you can see, we are introducing one of the most unusual new fantasy characters of all time— the SPIDER-MAN, who will appear every month in Amazing Fantasy, if your letters request it!

(GOODMAN enters)

GOODMAN
Stanley, we're canceling Amazing Fantasy.

STAN
What? But Spider-Man—

GOODMAN
Sales are rotten. It's dead.

(GOODMAN exits. GOLDBERG enters)

GOLDBERG
Um…Stan?

STAN
Yes Stan? What do you need?

GOLDBERG
Well...it's the coloring for...The Hulk...the gray is muddy...

STAN
Change it.

(GOLDBERG exits. STAN turns to JACK)

STAN
You win. The Hulk is green. How about that Norse mythology book you wanted to do?

JACK
Thor?

STAN
You thought I forgot, didn't you?

JACK
No. I thought you totally ignored me.

STAN
Forsooth! 'Tis the thundering might of the mighty Thor!...He's the God of Thunder, right?

JACK
This is a big idea. We run it out a few years, and smash everything with Ragnarok...then we start over with space-age replacements. New Gods, you might say.

STAN
Oh, but hey...don't get too crazy with the Gods stuff OK? We don't want to offend any of those pain-in-the-ass religious types. Just keep him fighting crooks, aliens and such. Ooh! Rock men from Jupiter!

(Projected: August, 1962)

(Projected: The cover of JOURNEY INTO MYSTERY #83, the premiere of Thor)

STAN
Thorr the mighty, all hail the greatest new super-hero of all time, who will appeareth regularly in Journey Into Mystery! Methinks thou shall call upon thine newsdealer to reserve next month's issue now! It's sure to selleth-out!

(*STAN looks around, FLO enters*)

FLO
What's the matter? You look nervous.

STAN
I'm waiting for Martin to pop out of the shadows and cancel this book, too!

(*FLO looks over his shoulder*)

(*Projected: The final panel of JOURNEY INTO MYSTERY #83, with a misspelling of "Thor"*)

FLO
I think Thor only has one "R," Stan.

STAN
One little mistake.

(*Lights shift. ROZ enters, and STAN once again addresses his readers*)

(*Projected: November, 1962*)

(*STAN performs*)

STAN
Look—enough of this 'Dear Editor' jazz from now on! Jolly Jack Kirby—

(*JACK waves over his shoulder. ROZ places a glass of milk next to him, and watches STAN*)

STAN

—and Smilin' Stan Lee (that's us!) read each and every letter personally! So we're laying down new orders for our fanatical followers, address your letters directly to "Stan and Jack." As it be written, so shall it be done!

ROZ

Well, at least he mentioned you first.

JACK

Once. Then it's back to "Stan and Jack, Stan and Jack."

(ROZ glances at Jack's drawing board)

ROZ

What's this? Mister Mount Rushmore?

JACK

I call this guy Darkseid.

(Projected: Jack's concept sketch for Darkseid)

JACK

I sorta don't want Stanley to see it. He'll want to throw him away, somebody for the Fantastic Four to beat on for a month.

ROZ

Kirby, don't you dare give this to Stanley Lieber. Don't you dare.

(ROZ exits)

(Projected: March, 1963)

STAN

Hey, Jackson! What do you think when I say arms manufacturer?

JACK

I think war profiteers are heartless bastards.

STAN
A heart condition! That's good stuff, Jackson! He builds something that keeps him alive AND makes him a hero.

JACK
Maybe a suit of armor? Arms, armor?

STAN
Bingo, Jackson!! Draw it up!

JACK
I'm doing three books a month as it is! I can't draw everything!

STAN
I can get Don Heck to finish it, but you do the design, and layout the first issue.

JACK
You gonna pay me for that?

STAN
We'll figure it out. C'mon, the iron is hot! Hey, hey, hey...that's a good name!

(Projected: The cover of TALES OF SUSPENSE #39, the intro of Iron Man)

JACK
You got a plot for me?

STAN
I have full faith in you, Jack! I've gotta gab with Ditko. Goodman saw the final sales numbers and wants more Spider-Man!

JACK
Well, isn't that just swell for you.

(Projected: May, 1963)

(Projected: The cover of THE FANTASTIC FOUR #14)

(STAN performs)

STAN
Have you noticed our new trade mark on the upper left hand corner of the very magazine you have, in your infinite good taste and unparalleled wisdom, in your sweaty mitts?

(Projected: The first Marvel Comics logo)

(The OBSERVER appears, and produces a "MAKE MINE MARVEL!!!" sign)

(Projected: a Kirby Krackle panel)

STAN
ALL our mags will be sporting this handsome insignia! When you see this logo, you'll know that mag has been crafted by the ink-stained hands and fevered brows of our…say it now, say it proud…Marvel Bullpen! With this mark, we can truly say that we, and you, our Merry Marvel Marching Society, have entered THE MARVEL AGE OF COMICS!!!

(Lights shift. The OBSERVER throws aside his robe to reveal a beanie hat and short pants)

(Projected; More Kirby Krackle)

(Lights fade out)

Scene Eleven

(Lights fade in. FLO sits at a reception desk, the door opens, and The OBSERVER, *channeling eleven-year-old Michael Uslan, enters the scene)*

(Projected: 575 Madison Ave, the offices of Marvel Comics)

OBSERVER
Where is it!?

FLO
Can I help you?

OBSERVER
Where's the Baxter Building? *(Waves a Fantastic Four comic book)* It's right here! It's in New York, and I want to see it!

FLO
Well, gosh. I hate to tell you, but the Baxter Building isn't a real place. Our writers and artists made it up.

OBSERVER
But it's right here in my comic! Everything else is real.

(STAN and JACK enter, arguing)

JACK
That wasn't the concept at all, Stanley! I keep giving you my best ideas, and then you turn 'em into oatmeal!

FLO
Boys! We have guests.

(JACK and STAN both notice the kid)

JACK
Aw, crimney! Sorry kid. Sometimes I blow my stack.

OBSERVER
Stan Lee? Really?

STAN
In the flesh, pardner! What's your handle? I gotta know our merry marchers by name...

OBSERVER
Michael.

(They shake hands)

STAN
Michael! "He who is likened to God!" Y'know what's EVEN BETTER? It's your lucky day, because this guy, right here? That's The King, himself!

OBSERVER
No way! Jack Kirby?

STAN
Look at that, Jackson! Our devoted public. Say, is it Michael, or just Mike?

OBSERVER
Mike!

STAN
That's what your friends call ya, don't they? 'Cause they're your pals! I know a guy, he always calls me "Stanley," when I like to be called "Stan." Now, WE'RE friends, right Mike? One big, happy Marveldom?

OBSERVER
You bet, Mister Lee!

STAN
Hey, now! What did we say about that? We're pals, Mike! None of that "Mister Lee" guff. I'm Stan, and this is Jack.

FLO
I was just about to get a couple of free books for Michael, er...Mike.

(She pulls out some comics and hands them to "MIKE")

STAN
That's a start Flo!

OBSERVER
Flo? Fabulous Flo Steinberg? You're as pretty as I imagined!

FLO
Why, thank you, Mike.

STAN
We can do better than a couple of free comics for such a devoted reader, and budding ladies man! How about a page of original King Kirby art for Mike, here?...what's your full handle, pardner?

OBSERVER
Mike Uslan!

JACK
Stanley, don't do that. That's my...

STAN
'Nuff said! Fix up our friend here with one of Jack's pages out of my office. Make it a good one! And a lifetime membership for Mike Uslan in the Merry Marvel Marching Society! Free of charge, of course.

JACK
Stanley? You're giving away my pages?

OBSERVER
Thanks, Stan!! You too, Mister Kirby!

STAN
Catch ya around, Mike!

(FLO leads The OBSERVER out)

JACK
What the hell are you doing?

STAN
What do you mean, Jackson?

JACK
That's MY art! You can't give it away. My blood, sweat and tears!

STAN
You drew it for the company, the company owns it, and I just used it to...hopefully...make a lifetime fan. That's our job, Jack!

(STAN exits)

JACK
You're the editor.

(Lights shift)

Scene Twelve

(Projected: January 1966)

(Lights shift to JACK in the basement, he strips off his shirt and sits at his drawing table. ROZ enters)

JACK
What'd the doc say?

ROZ
The asthma is getting worse. He said the best thing would be a warmer climate. Out west. Arizona, or California, maybe.

JACK
With the crazies?

ROZ
People are people, Jack. Just because they didn't grow up on Essex Street doesn't mean they're weird.

JACK
They ain't weird enough…Moving to Long Island felt like I was betraying the neighborhood, what the hell would the guys think if I ran off ta La-La land?

ROZ
It'd help Lisa, Kirby...What did Stanley say about the art?

JACK
Goodman's line. The company owns the pages after I turn 'em in. It's always been that way. Hell, Simon and I never turned art back to nobody.

ROZ
Those kids keep writing. Selling those pages could really help us out.

JACK
I'll send 'em sketches. They're fans, they don't need to pay. They've already paid for this house and everything else. I like getting the letters with the sketches. Some of 'em ain't half bad.

ROZ
You're their hero. And mine. *(Kisses him)* I laid out a clean blazer for tomorrow. My man is going to look snappy for the press.

JACK
Ah, crap. That Herald-Trib thing? The damn book's already plotted. Stan just wants to dog and pony for this guy.

ROZ
Don't be that way, Kirby. The one time they want to talk with you, and not just Stanley, and I am proud of you. *(Smacks his shoulder)* Just be nice, Kirby! Turn on the charm for once in your life.

JACK
What charm?

ROZ
That's what my mother said.

(They kiss, she exits, and JACK goes back to his page. Lights fade out)

Scene Thirteen

(STAN enters with NAT FREEDLAND, a reporter for the New York Herald-Tribune)

STAN
Welcome to the world-famous Marvel Bullpen, Nat!

FREEDLAND
So this is where the pow and zap happens?

STAN
Well, we like to think we have more to offer than that. Tell ya what, would you like to sit in on a plotting session with myself and my best artist? See how the sausage is made?

FREEDLAND
That's what I'm here for, Mr Lee.

STAN
Hey, I tell you what...Call me Stan.

(JACK enters)

STAN
Jackson!

JACK
Stanley.

(STAN gives JACK a look)

STAN
Nat, THIS is the world's greatest comic book artist, Jack "The King" Kirby! He's been my right-hand man in building Marvel.

JACK
We're partners.

STAN
That's what I just said, Jackson! This is Nat Freedland, he's doing the article for the Herald-Tribune. He's looking to sit in on our plotting session.

(Projected: The Masthead for the NEW YORK HERALD-TRIBUNE)

JACK
Fine.

(Beat)

STAN
Jack's a man of few words. That's why I do the writing.

JACK
Some of it.

FREEDLAND
I love your work, Mister Kirby. Pop art masterworks.

STAN
Hey, we're all friends here, it's Stan and Jack!

JACK
Or Jack and Stan.

(JACK and FREEDLAND take seats, JACK pulls a drawing board onto his lap, FREEDLAND makes notes)

FREEDLAND
Just act like I'm not here.

STAN
How can I do that? I love an audience!

JACK
Can we get on with this?

(STAN doesn't sit)

STAN
Ok, so where were we?

JACK
The Surfer.

STAN
Right! So, the Silver Surfer's been off in space since he helped the FF stop Galactus...

FREEDLAND
Galactus? Silver Surfer?

STAN
A giant space traveler, cosmically powered.

JACK
He's a god. The Surfer is his herald.

STAN
Well, of a sort.

JACK
That's MY concept.

STAN
He's coming in the March issue. Our latest magnum opus, right, Jack?

JACK
The FF fights God.

STAN
Weeeell, sort of. We'll make sure you get copies, Nat.

FREEDLAND
Can't wait to read them.

(STAN returns to "plotting")

STAN
Suppose Alicia...That's The Thing's blind girlfriend, Nat...is in some kind of trouble, and the Silver Surfer hangs ten in to help..."

(STAN begins to act out the action. FREEDLAND turns and addresses the audience)

FREEDLAND
Lee starts pacing and gesturing, warming up.

STAN
The Thing sees them together, gets the wrong idea, and BANG! A big fight with the Surfer.

FREEDLAND
Stan Lee reminds one of Rex Harrison, ultra-Madison Avenue, handsome with eyes that convey humor and warmth. He sports a rich suntan, highlighting the brightest-colored ivy wardrobe in captivity.

JACK
Ummh.

FREEDLAND
The King is a middle-aged man, sucking a huge green cigar, the cloud of smoke swirling over his baggy eyes and a Robert Hall-ish suit. If you caught him on the subway, you'd say, "that's the assistant foreman in a girdle factory."

STAN
Meanwhile, the Fantastic Four is in deep, deep trouble.
Doctor Doom has...

FREEDLAND
I love Doctor Doom! Fantastic stuff.

(STAN laughs)

STAN
We didn't pull the title out of the air, did we Jack?...The
nefarious Victor Von Doom has caught our heroes again,
and they need the Thing's help!

FREEDLAND
Lee is at full power, now. Throwing punches, and himself,
into the world of imagination.

*(STAN does so, jumping on top of his desk. JACK rolls his
eyes)*

JACK
Right.

FREEDLAND
Kirby has kind of a high-pitched voice.

STAN
Alicia makes The Thing realize his terrible mistake. His
greatest fear, to lose control and clobber somebody for
no reason!

FREEDLAND
Ah! Clobberin' Time.

STAN
That's right! IT'S CLOBBERIN' TIME!!

*(JACK nods unenthusiastically. STAN jumps from his
desk)*

STAN
The Thing is brokenhearted, too ashamed to face his girl or his family. But they need him, and he's failing them for a second time!

FREEDLAND
Lee sags back on his desk, spent.

(STAN does so)

JACK
Great.

(FREEDLAND looks at JACK, waiting for more, which does not come)

FREEDLAND
Kirby has leaped out of the chair he was crumpled in.

(He looks at JACK again. Nothing)

FREEDLAND
The cigar is out of his mouth and his baggy eyes are aglow.

(Another look)

JACK
Great.

(JACK puts his drawing board aside)

FREEDLAND
His high voice is young with enthusiasm.

(STAN springs back to life)

STAN
Will that work for you, Nat?

FREEDLAND
I think I have what I need, Stan.

(Lights shift. STAN and JACK exit)

(Projected: The "Super Heroes With Super-Problems" article)

FREEDLAND
Here's the beating heart of the Marvel Age of Comics, in the form of Stan 'The Man' Lee.

(Lights shift)

Scene Fourteen

(Darkened stage, ROZ enters in a robe. A newspaper is thrown on stage. She waves and picks it up, opens it and flips pages, then stops cold)

ROZ
Oh no. No!

(She walks to a phone and picks it up, dials. Across the stage, a phone rings, and a light comes up as STAN enters)

STAN
I hope this is an emergency, calling this early on Sunday morning.

ROZ
You are a tiny little man, Stanley Lieber. A tiny little man.

STAN
What? Roz?

ROZ
How could you do this to Jack? To my Kirby?

STAN

Roz, I don't know...

ROZ

"An assistant foreman in a girdle factory?!"

STAN

I have no idea what you're talking about.

ROZ

This is your doing, and I will NEVER forgive you, Stanley. You're nothing but a...a...a...Funky Flashman!

STAN

Roz, but I...Is this about the interview? I haven't even...

ROZ

As God as my witness, I will never let you, or anyone else take advantage of my Kirby again. Do you understand that, Stanley?

(JOAN enters behind STAN)

JOAN

Who calls at seven AM on a Sunday?

STAN

Roz, Jack's my partner, I would never do anything to...

ROZ

From now on, my only concern is with Jack and our family, no one else!

(ROZ slams the phone down. STAN winces and pulls the receiver from his ear)

JOAN

What's the matter?

STAN

It was Roz Kirby...She wanted me to look at the paper.

(Lights out on STAN and JOAN, and exit. JACK enters behind ROZ. She wads the newspaper up and hides it)

JACK
Babe, what are you yellin' about in here?

ROZ
It's all right Kirby. I just need a new frying pan.

JACK
You break it when you cracked me in the head last time?

(ROZ laughs)

ROZ
Well, I told you to stay out of my kitchen.

JACK
You're the boss…You seen that newspaper? The article's supposed to be in it today.

ROZ
The boy ain't been by yet.

JACK
Don't that figure. The one day I'm lookin' for some good news. What a revoltin' development.

(JACK exits. ROZ looks at the crumpled newsprint)

ROZ
Ain't that the truth.

(Lights shift)

END OF ACT ONE

<hr>

ACT II

<hr>

SCENE ONE

(Lights shift. The OBSERVER returns)

(Projected: Spacescape)

OBSERVER
Space. An infinite, suffocating void of blackness with achingly momentary, dazzling spectacles of cosmic majesty in the corner of one's eye.

(He briefly glances at the space image)

OBSERVER
Believe me, after a few billion years? This cosmic thing's a real grind.

(Lights up on STAN, primping in a chair, freshly adorned with a toupee)

(Projected: 1967)

OBSERVER
Likewise, the more Stan Lee worked to forge the bonds of fandom. His expert embellishment forged the fantasy

of "Stan the Man," "Jolly Jack," and the entire "Mighty Marvel Bullpen." Yet the more he found himself outside the glare of true fame, trapped by the essence of his enterprise. The wide, mainstream accolades and adulation he dreamed of in his youth…painfully elude his grasp.

(Lights shift. The OBSERVER exits. SUZIE SUTTON, very much an undergraduate broadcasting major, enters and sits opposite STAN. There is some canned music and bad lighting)

(Projected: The Virginia Tech Seal)

ANNOUNCER *(Off stage or recorded)*
Welcome back to Virginia Tech Television! Bringing you the best in Hokie news and entertainment! Produced in cooperation with Blacksburg Public Access Television. Now here's your host, Suzie Sutton!

SUZIE
Hello…Today in the studio we have with us…

(She checks her notes)

SUZIE
Mister Stan Lee who is the editor of Marvel Comics…

(Again with the notes)

SUZIE
And he's going to tell us about how he got started… Now, Stan, um, the Marvel Age of Comics…

STAN
That's what we like to call it! A revolution the history of literature, as we all know.

(STAN chuckles, SUZIE gives an weak smile)

SUZIE
It started in 1961 with the, uh, Fantastic Four? How'd you come up with that?

STAN
Well, I tell ya, Suzie...Can I call you Suzie?

SUZIE
Sure.

STAN
Well, I was the head writer. Now, that doesn't mean I wrote heads...

SUZIE
(Weak chuckle) OK.

STAN
I was the chief writer. The ridiculous notion was let's try to inject some realism into the fantasy, and the juxtaposition seems to have a struck a chord.

SUZIE
With the people?

STAN
With the more intelligent people!

SUZIE
How did you develop your concept?

STAN
Well, we work a little differently from other publishers. Traditionally, comic books were written very much like a play, with the dialogue and action all laid out. Well, in the beginning, if I may put on my deepest voice and invoke Genesis...

(No reaction)

STAN
I was writing most of the stories, and I was having trouble keeping up with the artists, so Jack Kirby, who we like to call "The King," and I...

SUZIE
Unfortunately, we're out of time.

STAN
Really?

SUZIE
Stay tuned for Mass for Shut-ins, and I'll be back tomorrow with...

(She checks her notes again)

SUZIE
...the state champion debate club. Thank you for enlightening us today...

(She's lost her place in her notes)

SUZIE
...Mister McFee.

(STAN is caught in the headlights. Lights shift. SUZIE exits as JOAN enters dressed for an evening out)

JOAN
Come on, Stan. We have dinner with the dean.

STAN
Another week, another edition of, "so, you write for children and morons."

JOAN
Don't be a pill. You have an image to keep up.

STAN
I was supposed to be a real writer. I should be in Hollywood. I could make movies!

JOAN
You're my beloved husband, Stan The Man Lee, the face of a major publisher...

STAN
A major comic book publisher.

JOAN
...An icon beloved by all your fans. They know who you are, just like I do. Now, you need to change, the dean and his wife are waiting.

(SUZIE enters, speaking as she crosses the stage)

SUZIE
Great interview, Mister Ailey, good luck with the cartoons!

(She exits)

STAN
I think I'm losing my mind.

(JOAN kisses his cheek)

JOAN
I knew that when you flew to Reno.

(JOAN and STAN exit. Lights shift)

Scene Two

(MARTIN GOODMAN sits behind a desk, he stands, and waves someone into the light)

GOODMAN
Jack! It's fantastic to see you, come in.

JACK
Martin.

GOODMAN
How are Roz and the kids?

JACK
They're fine.

GOODMAN
That wife of yours is a force of nature.

JACK
Then make her happy, give me my art back.

GOODMAN
I give you your art, I have to give everyone...

JACK

You could if you wanted to.

(Beat)

GOODMAN

Stanley tells me that you're pulling up stakes and heading out west. How are you doing on moving expenses?

JACK

That's none of your damn business.

GOODMAN

I know how important it is to get...

(GOODMAN checks a note on his desk)

GOODMAN

...Lisa to a warmer climate. I'm thinking that we could arrange a loan.

JACK

But you can't give me my art back?

GOODMAN

I don't see any reason to worry about interest, or anything like that. You're family.

JACK

I am? First I've heard of it. Sounds ta me like you need somethin'.

GOODMAN

We have a bit of a...conflict with Joe Simon.

(Lights shift, and JOE SIMON is revealed)

(Projected: The first page of CAPTAIN AMERICA COMICS #1)

SIMON

I created Captain America in 1940 with my partner at

the time, Jack Kirby. The character was not, in any way, a work-for-hire. We shopped it around, and it was picked up by Martin Goodman's publishing house, Timely Comics, now known as Marvel. Captain America is my creation, and it's current use by Marvel Comics infringes on my right to renew the copyright in my name.

(Projected: The Simon and Kirby byline)

(Lights shift back. GOODMAN produces a letter)

GOODMAN
What we need is for you to sign this letter, saying that you and Joe created Captain America as work for hire at Timely.

JACK
That's not true.

GOODMAN
Jack, please understand, we intend to compensate Mister Simon, and you. It's only fair, you co-created the character.

JACK
You're Goddamn right.

GOODMAN
But these issues of ownership? Need to be put to bed.

JACK
You want me to rat out the guy who was my partner for a decade?

GOODMAN
I want you to help yourself, Jack. Marvel wants a better life for your family.

(Lights shift, GOODMAN exits and ROZ enters)

JACK
I know we could use that cash, Roz.

ROZ
Joe should of talked to you. Why does everyone go behind your back?

JACK
I can't believe he was gonna get his cut, and leave me out like yesterday's garbage. I won't. In the old days, I could set things ta rights sockin' a guy in the kisser... I'd feel better anyway.

(Beat)

JACK
They're gonna cut a deal. It's not like Simon'll get nothin'. It'd sure make movin' easier.

(Lights shift)

Scene Three

(Projected: 1968)

(STAN is working in his office. The door opens and GOODMAN enters)

STAN
Martin! How the heck are ya.

GOODMAN
Mister Goodman, Stanley. Have you heard from Kirby yet?

STAN
Not since they moved. Even Jack's gonna need a couple of days to settle in out there.

GOODMAN
You let me know when he sends in his first pages.

STAN
Right-o!

GOODMAN
It's going to be vital in the next few weeks to make sure the business is operating as expected.

STAN
Another audit?

GOODMAN
Stanley, are you a company man? I need to know. Right
now.

STAN
How could you even ask me that Mar...Mister Goodman?
I've always been loyal.

GOODMAN
There's an offer from Perfect Film and Chemical.

STAN
Who?

GOODMAN
I'm selling the company. We needed to shore up all the
copyright issues. Kirby made short work of Joe Simon's
claim, and I just want to make sure we won't have any
other problems. Perfect thinks that your presence is
important.

STAN
I have no intention of biting the hand that feeds me.

GOODMAN
I'm going to stay on as publisher to transition, and then
Chip is going to take over.

STAN
But I thought...

GOODMAN
He's my son, and I am going to provide for his future.

STAN
I thought you'd look out for me.

GOODMAN
Stanley, I've spent the last twenty years looking out for

you, you're family, but you're not my son. Don't tell the staff until it's public.

(GOODMAN exits. STAN sits alone. Lights shift and JOAN enters)

JOAN
Stan, I have a new lamp I am looking at. It's an Artemide.

STAN
Should I know what that means?

JOAN
It's Italian.

STAN
Do we own anything that isn't?

JOAN
Only you, my love.

(They kiss. STAN is preoccupied)

JOAN
What's the matter?

STAN
Martin's selling the company.

JOAN
There's no chance they'll let you go. You are Marvel Comics.

STAN
My presence is apparently required for the deal, but not enough for a promotion. Chip Goodman is gonna be my boss.

JOAN
Chip Goodman is an idiot.

STAN

I just...I thought I'd be publisher when Martin was ready to go.

JOAN

You turned his entire company around, and he's insulting you.

(JOAN pulls STAN to her)

JOAN

Listen to me, Stan Lee...You remember this when you go in to negotiate with these new people. You made this company, your voice is the voice of Marvel.

STAN

I should've quit this business fifteen years ago.

JOAN

Oh, stop it! Only you could whine about this. Are you famous?

STAN

I wouldn't say...

JOAN

Are you lecturing at colleges? Are you revered and loved by your audience?

STAN

A bunch of silly little stories for kids.

JOAN

You're setting their expectations for the world, for progress, for justice and responsibility. You're changing the world, little by little. You're Stan Lee! You ARE Marvel Comics!

(JOAN gets up and begins to exit. Then turns back)

JOAN
We'll talk about the lamp later.

(*JOAN exits. Lights shift*)

(*Projected: Stan's Soapbox!*)

(*STAN reflects for a moment, then turns to the audience*)

STAN
For those of you keeping track at home, it's been almost a decade since the Marvel Age of Comics first exploded upon the unsuspecting literary world! Whatever we are, Merry Marchers, you've made us! We BELIEVE in our swingin' super-types! Our fearless fables are what's happening, true believers! The REAL world? That's what we have doubts about! Until next month, FACE FRONT! It's where the action is! EXCELSIOR!!!"

(*Lights shift*)

Scene Four

(The OBSERVER steps into view)

(Projected: The Kirby Home at 2590 Sapra Street in Thousand Oaks CA)

OBSERVER
A Continent away, the King of Comics finds a new home, a new life, and a door opened. Opened to a world built of experience, enthusiasm, and sheer imagination. A hidden world of new heroes and epic evil. A grand, idiosyncratic world that could only, in it's purity... and peculiarity, spring from Jack Kirby's unbridled imagination.

(Projected: THOUSAND OAKS, CA — 1971)

(Lights shift. ROZ enters with CARMINE INFANTINO, venerated artist, and new editor-in-chief of DC Comics)

INFANTINO
I gotta tell ya, Roz, it's really nice of you and Jack to have me for dinner. I don't know a soul in California.

ROZ
Oh, Jack'll love to see an old face, Carmine. He misses
New York so much.

INFANTINO
All day playing yes-sir no-sir with these Warner Brothers
bigwigs. Talkin' to these LA-LA land folks is like havin'
a conversation with a french poodle.

ROZ
Jack thought moving out here might open some doors in
Hollywood, but these people are so two-faced. At least
you have some pull.

INFANTINO
Aw, hell, Roz. Most of these guys don't even know they
own DC comics, let alone who's running editorial.

(JACK enters)

JACK
Carmine Infantino! Who let you out of the gorilla cage?

(The two men embrace)

INFANTINO
Look at this guy, all tanned up and gone California.

JACK
Oh ho! And look at mister Editor in Chief.

INFANTINO
Editorial Director.

JACK
What the hell does that mean?

INFANTINO
Corporate types love to make up new titles. And ta think,
I started out workin' for you!

(They laugh)

JACK

Yeah, isn't that a kick in the head.

ROZ

Jack and Joe treated all of you like family.

INFANTINO

Oh, c'mon Roz. If by family you mean child labor.

ROZ

I didn't invite you here to insult my husband, Carmine!

INFANTINO

Hey, hey…That was one of the happiest times of my life! But hell, Jack, you know better'n me how those shops worked. It's always about swingin' the best deal.

(Beat)

JACK

You ain't here for old times, Infantino. What do you need? Take your shot or get off the pot.

INFANTINO

I heard things were rough with Stan and Goodman. Maybe we could find a place for ya?

ROZ

He can't go back to DC, not after that garbage with Jack Schiff.

INFANTINO

Schiff is long gone. Liebowitz is still publisher, and he figures if you up and moved to California, you might be willing to up and move in other ways.

ROZ

What you pay? Jack is a talent, and he deserves the best.

INFANTINO

I will guarantee we can beat whatever Goodman is

feeding you. I got the best writers lined up to work with you, the best editors to oversee the material.

JACK
I don't want to work with any writers, I don't want any editors messing with my books either. I want to control my own work.

INFANTINO
You want to draw, and write, and edit?

ROZ
He's done it all before.

JACK
I've been stuck behind Joe Simon and Stanley Lieber for too long.

INFANTINO
Jack, I don't know if I can promise that.

ROZ
Then you don't want Kirby.

JACK
I don't want anyone else taking credit. These ideas are the best I've ever had, and they are mine, period. Carmine, I have so many ideas it'll make your head spin. A whole new world of heroes and villains, Gods and monsters. A Fourth World.

INFANTINO
What the hell is the Fourth World?

ROZ
His masterpiece.

INFANTINO
Jack you better show me what you have.

(Projected: The cover of THE NEW GODS #1)

JACK
It starts with the epilogue.

INFANTINO
The epilogue? That's the end...

(The lights shift as JACK begins to speak)

(Projected: a series of "Kirby krackle" panel sections as JACK speaks)

JACK
There came a time when the old gods died! A fiery holocaust consuming all, the brave, cunning and noble! This was the last day, a maelstrom of unspeakable power, the final moment. Rending the home of the old gods with a blinding death flash reaching across the cosmos. All that remained were two molten bodies, spinning, barren and clean, awash in the echo of intergalactic thunder.

(Projected: An image of Supertown, paradise, heaven)

JACK
Supertown of New Genesis! An oasis, a utopia of truth, beauty, learning and peace. Where every blight has been overcome under the benevolent gaze and gentle wisdom of Highfather. The home of the New Gods!

(Projected: Apokolips)

JACK
But every light must cast a shadow, and for New Genesis, it is Apokolips! Awash in absolute darkness feeding upon the downtrodden denizens and the world itself!

(Projected: a silhouette of Darkseid)

JACK
The domain of the great Darkseid! An armed camp where life is evil and anti-life is the great goal!

(Beat. Lights shift to normal)

INFANTINO
Great. What does it mean?

JACK
Give me a decent contract, give me control, give me my art back...

(The OBSERVER gestures to the projection screen)

(Projected: "The Great One is Coming" DC Comics Ad)

JACK
...And I'll show you.

(Lights shift)

Scene Five

(Lights shift. A cocktail party, STAN, now fully evolved into his toupee-mustache-sunglasses image, is standing with JOAN, in a fancy evening dress, both holding martinis)

(Projected: LONG ISLAND — 1972)

STAN
Now, this is what I've been waiting for.

JOAN
Cheers, my love!

(They clink their glasses together)

STAN
Here's to the future!

JOAN
Yes. Stan Lee, publisher!

STAN
Stan "The Man" Lee presents Marvel Comics!

(GREER GRANT enters)

GREER
Oh, here we are! The Lees themselves! I am so happy I ran into you.

JOAN
Why Greer! So lovely to see you again.

STAN
Greer...Grant? Isn't it?

JOAN
Oh, Stan, you remember Miss Grant. She was the one so interested in my Gio Ponti...for about a minute.

GREER
(Laughs) Oh, Joan! I always love your deliciously wicked humor!

STAN
It's why I married her!

JOAN
Well, how are things at the South Shore Record? I wouldn't know, myself...

GREER
Well things are looking...

JOAN
...I only read the papers from the city.

(Beat)

GREER
I see.

STAN
Well, I tell ya, Greer. It's just lovely to be here at Martin's retirement party. Now that Cadence Industries is holding the reins, I suspect that...

JOAN
Oh Stan, I can see Greer eying my dress. Halston... authentic.

(MARTIN GOODMAN enters)

STAN
Martin!

GOODMAN
Stanley.

STAN
I am glad you stopped by, Martin. I wanted to tell you that you will be missed down at the office.

GOODMAN
Is that so?

STAN
Of course it is!

JOAN
(To GREER) Greer, will you be a darling and run along?

GREER
Well, I was hoping to ask Martin...

JOAN
I will give you a call if I have a garage sale.

GREER
Well!

(GREER exits in a huff)

STAN
I tell ya, Martin. It does my heart good to know that you'll be able to relax a bit.

JOAN
I'm sure Jean will be so pleased to have you all to herself.

GOODMAN
Stanley, I'm going to speak frankly, and then I'd like you to leave my house and never darken my door again.

STAN
What? Martin, we're family...

GOODMAN
Mister Goodman!...You went behind my back. I groomed Chip to take over for me, and you stole it from him.

JOAN
Martin, I can't believe...

GOODMAN
Mister Goodman! You silly little woman!

STAN
Mar...Mister Goodman, I didn't go behind anyone's back! You sold the company to Cadence, and they offered me the job. I didn't ask for it!

GOODMAN
Save the fiction for the funny books, Stanley.

JOAN
Stan has worked night and day for you!

STAN
It's okay, Joan. Leave it. We'll go.

(STAN extends his hand)

STAN
I wish you well.

(GOODMAN looks at the offered handshake)

GOODMAN
I just found out that Jack Kirby signed a contract with Jack Liebowitz and Carmine Infantino over at DC...

STAN
What?

GOODMAN
...So, I'll just wish you luck.

JOAN
I don't believe Jack Kirby is a traitor.

GOODMAN
(*Laughs*) Jack Kirby sold out Joe Simon for about five thousand dollars. And, Joan? I don't think you should blame Jack for the very tactic that your husband used to prompt Cadence to pass over my son.

JOAN
I don't know..

GOODMAN
Seems Stanley met with Carmine, too. It's business, but I take my business very personally.

STAN
Martin...

GOODMAN
MISTER GOODMAN!! Now get out.

(*GOODMAN and JOAN exit. The lights shift, and STAN turns to the audience*)

(*Projected: Stan's Soapbox masthead*)

STAN
Sad news from the Bullpen my friends, as of the time of this writing, Jack 'The King' Kirby has unexpectedly announced his resignation from our surprised and stalwart little staff...That's where we're at, under-staffed, but as bushy-tailed as ever!

(STAN stops for a moment and reflects before pushing forward)

STAN
While we're at it, if you'll allow me a moment of personal grandiosity, yours truly has been named publisher of all of Marveldom as of this very issue you hold in your hot little hands! So, watch the sparks fly, friend, as we passionately prepare some of the wildest and wackiest surprises to electrify your eyeballs and stagger your senses! Hang loose! Face front! Here comes phase two, all for you! EXCELSIOR!!

(Lights shift)

Scene Six

(Projected: "Kirby is Here" DC comics ad)

(Lights shift. JACK sits at his drawing board, the phone rings. ROZ enters and answers the phone)

(Projected: THOUSAND OAKS — 1972)

ROZ
Kirby residence.

(Lights up on INFANTINO, on the phone in his New York office)

INFANTINO
Roz! How the hell are ya?

ROZ
Carmine! I'm fantastic.

INFANTINO
Kids doing well?

ROZ
Lisa is running around like a wildcat, the move did wonders for her.

INFANTINO

Really glad to hear that, Roz. Y'know I gotta talk to Jack right? As much as I love your voice.

ROZ

Don't you try to flirt with me, Infantino. I know your type.

INFANTINO

I know he's there, he never leaves the basement!

ROZ

(Laughs) He's committed, working for the best publisher in the business. *(Pulls the phone aside)* Jack! Your boss is on the phone!

(JACK looks up, and grabs a phone)

JACK

Just walk downstairs! Don't waste the dime to tell me to shape up.

ROZ

It's Carmine, you wisenheimer!

(JACK chuckles to himself, and puts the receiver to his ear)

JACK

You sweet-talkin' my wife again, Infantino?

INFANTINO

Every chance I get! Calling on business, Jack. We gotta talk about your books.

JACK

I'm working on eleven now.

(Projected: The cover of THE NEW GODS #11)

INFANTINO

Yeah. You gotta wrap it up there.

(Beat)

JACK
What?

INFANTINO
It's canceled. Sales have been dropping. It ain't worth it anymore. You can keep Mister Miracle going for now, it's doing better than the others.

JACK
Carmine, this is my...

INFANTINO
Yeah, we know. It's not selling. I don't know what to tell you Jack, the kids aren't taking to your "Dark Sid."

JACK
Darkseid.

INFANTINO
Sure, whatever. Look we talked about a couple of other things. Fox screwed us on the Planet of the Apes rights, but Liebowitz still liked that "last boy on Earth" pitch. Now. I have to say this...I know you want to work alone, but we'd like to hook you up with a scripter. DC likes a...little more polish in the dialogue.

JACK
I don't work with writers anymore.

INFANTINO
The letters we're getting...they're not that positive. EVERYBODY loves the art. You're the King, we all know that.

JACK
I ain't seeing no negative letters.

INFANTINO
(Sighs) Jack, we've been holding the worst back.

(Lights shift. The OBSERVER appears in costuming that suggests a college professor)

OBSERVER
I have managed to keep up with New Gods, somehow. The most obvious handicap is Kirby's amateurish dialogue. "I feel! I anger! I fight!" Or "It stems from the waves of the mind." Can you explain what that's supposed to mean? And what's with all the random quotation marks?

(Lights shift. The OBSERVER exits)

INFANTINO
So, we want to assign a writer to you. Denny O'Neil expressed interest. He's a real wiz, bright young kid. I think you two can do something special.

(Silence)

INFANTINO
Look I know how you feel…

JACK
Lemme explain it to you like back in the neighborhood, Infantino. Ain't nobody gonna scam their way into havin' a claim to what I do! If you want me to work with a writer, fine! You have them send me a complete script, page by page, panel by panel, and I'll draw the damn thing as I'm told.

INFANTINO
No one's saying anything about your art or storytelling. We all know who you are.

JACK
Do you? Do you know who I am, and what I've done? I came to DC…

(ROZ enters, and stands silently watching her husband)

INFANTINO
Now you hold on one damn second! You came to DC for more money, benefits, and we're not running off and throwing your art in a warehouse like Marvel did. You're getting as much, if not more, respect from me and this company as any professional.

JACK
I don't think you...

INFANTINO
So be a Goddamn professional! We let you run with this. It didn't sell the way we wanted, so we're canceling it. That's the editorial decision. That's MY decision.

JACK
This was my masterpiece.

INFANTINO
Ah, cut the crap, Kirby. We gave you a better deal than Goodman, because we respect you. Let me tell you, no one over here regrets it.

(Beat)

JACK
You're the editor.

INFANTINO
We've all had books canceled, Jack. All we're saying is... come up with something else. Maybe another super-soldier thing?

JACK
Right, fine. One man army.

INFANTINO
Look, Jack. I'm sorry. I know these books meant a lot

to you... I'll let you work independent, OK? No writer, no editor. You got three years left on your contract. That last boy thing is fine for one, or that horror thing? The Demon? Whatever.

(Short beat)

INFANTINO
It's just business, Jack. Best to Roz and the kids, OK?

(INFANTINO hangs up, his light goes out)

JACK
They take everything, Roz. Squander it all. Marvel shoved my life's work into a warehouse to rot. Now The New Gods are dead.

(Projected: The cover of THE NEW GODS #11 crumbles or burns)

(ROZ steps forward and puts a hand on JACK's shoulder)

ROZ
I love you, Kirby. You're my hero. Always and forever.

(Lights shift)

Scene Seven

(Lights shift, and the OBSERVER enters)

(Projected: The Marvel Comics Convention 1975 Program cover. It spins quickly)

OBSERVER
Thus spins the wheel of history. 'Round and 'round it goes.

(The projection comes to stop so as to be readable)

OBSERVER
For Jack Kirby, his bid to forge his own path left him traveling in a circle. He learned the hard lesson that history...

(Projected: NEW YORK CITY — 1975)

OBSERVER
...is often a matter of repetition.

(Lights shift. STAN is standing at a podium)

STAN

Here we are the very first IN PERSON gathering of the Merry Marvel Marchers! The assembled army of Marveldom! Welcome! Welcome all.

(Cheers from the crowd)

STAN

And, if you like this sensational soirée, we'll keep having them. As long as you keep buying tickets, that is!

(Laughs)

STAN

And let me tell you, friends, I hope you've picked up my latest opus, Origins of Marvel Comics!

(STAN holds up a copy of the book)

(Projected: THE ORIGINS OF MARVEL COMICS cover)

STAN

The real, uncensored truth on how your ol' pal Stan created Marvel Comics! It's dynamite, page after page of behind-the-scenes bombshells, and every word is true! I outta know, I WROTE IT!...And here's a little scoop for you all, there's not just one sequel on the way, but two!

(Cheers)

STAN

But, y'know true believers, I have to admit, as much as I like to take credit, and slap my name on everything.

(Laughs)

STAN

I couldn't have done it without one tremendously talented man, and all of you fans here, you lucky dogs, are in store for a real treat.

(There is a hush from the crowd)

STAN
But this news is too big to hold off for another minute! Jolly Jack Kirby is Back! THE KING IS BACK!!

(The crowd goes absolutely wild. JACK enters, waving)

STAN
That's right! Ol' King Kirby has returned to the bosom of the blushin' bullpen! And don't you forget, it was at Marvel where that title was bestowed!

JACK
That's what you tell me.

STAN
This is where his heart is. This is where it all started! And this is where one of the greatest talents in comics belongs!

JACK
I'm happy to be back, Stanley.

(Beat)

STAN
After all these years, Jackson, you, of all people, can call me Stan...Well, I know you're all just dying to know what The King will be working on. There will be a new series about the Gods that walk among us.

JACK
I call it The Eternals.

STAN
But better than that! He'll be the driving force behind the one and only Captain America! Returning to the character he created back in 1941!

(Cheers)

STAN
Say a few words, Jack!

JACK
Whatever I do at Marvel, I can assure you it will electrocute you in the mind!

STAN
Electrify, Jack. Electrify!

(The lights shift and the crowd fades to silence. STAN and JACK walk away from the podium, and meet JOAN and ROZ)

JOAN
Roz, I just love your dress! Where on Earth did you get something so unique?

ROZ
This old thing? Gee, I dunno, Joan. Sears?

JOAN
Sears? Really?

ROZ
I think so.

JOAN
Well, this is a Missoni. Neiman Marcus. Let's do some shopping while you're here! The boys will have work.

ROZ
I think I'd rather just stay with Jack.

JOAN
Oh, Roz! We could all have dinner, see a show! Wouldn't you enjoy a night on the town?

STAN
That was just terrific, Jack! Terrific! Everyone is so glad to have you back!

JACK
It seems like the kids are excited.

STAN
Why wouldn't they be? Stan and Jack, together again!

ROZ
Jack, let's go.

STAN
This is the start of a new era for us! We were a great team! We should do a project. Simon and Schuster has an offer on the table for a Silver Surfer book.

JACK
Team? Y'know, it's funny how you say that now, but when you write your little books, it sounds like you're a one-man band.

JOAN
Stan, let's not get involved with this.

JACK
Not get involved? Goodman's houseboy here NEVER gets involved, otherwise he might've grown a backbone and given my artwork back! He might've spoke up when they made me sign away all my characters just to put food on the table!

STAN
Jack, I don't own any of these characters either! I don't own a thing. I've got nothing to do with the art, it's company policy, talk to Cadence.

ROZ
But you're the face of Marvel Comics!

JACK
I got kids telling me about a warehouse full of my pages, and some schmuck telling them to tear 'em up or burn 'em as some sort of loyalty test!

STAN

Joanie, I just don't understand...

JOAN

These people are ungrateful, and you don't need...

ROZ

I'm sorry, what?

JACK

Roz, let it go, it's not worth it.

ROZ

Do you know anything about anything, you terrible woman!? My Kirby was a king when Stanley was cleaning out pencil sharpeners! Your ridiculous husband been riding Jack's coattails since 1941!

JOAN

King Kirby? It was my Stan who came up with that!

STAN

Ok, that's enough.

JACK

Roz, please.

JOAN

I'm going to the car.

(JOAN exits)

STAN

Joanie just looks out for me, Roz. Surely you understand that.

(No answer)

STAN

Jack. I am really happy you're back with us. You belong at Marvel. I'll do what you want, stay out of your way.

If I can do anything about the art, I will.

(STAN exits)

ROZ
His ego takes up so much room in that heart of his, I don't know how he has room to breathe.

(She exits. JACK reflects for a moment, then follows. Lights shift)

Scene Eight

STAN
Hey, hey True Believers! The greatest Marvel album of all is finally on sale! "Spider-Man: Rock Reflections of a Superhero!" It's got a doozy of a cover by Jazzy John Romita, and scintillating narration by a dashing wordsmith you MIGHT be familiar with! Just wait until you hear "No One's Got a Crush on Peter," and "Peter Stays and Spider-Man Goes," along with the other wooly wonderments on this dazzlin' disk! Remember! It's not a kiddie album. It's honest-to-Aunt-May rock and roll, performed by some of the best in the biz!!

(Projected: 1976)

(Lights shift. JACK is at his drawing board)

(Projected: The cover of THE ETERNALS #1)

JACK
The Gods are only the best of ourselves. We ask what's happening. When we say, "I know what's happening," as soon as we say that...Our egos are projected and we become gods.

(Lights shift, the OBSERVER appears in full-on stereotypical fanboy mode)

OBSERVER
Grandiose large-scale Kirby epics simply no longer work. They take months to tell a skimpy, over-simplified story. Lacking, both in storytelling and characterization. Stan Lee gave each and every character a motivation, love, fear, grudges...Jack Kirby's world is devoid of such things.

(Projected: The cover of CAPTAIN AMERICA #193)

JACK
The Captain America story I'm telling is Cap as he should be, slanted toward the bicentennial. I believe everyone will follow it closely. A novel of many chapters, each a different story, with The climax at the bicentennial.

(Lights shift back to the Fanboy OBSERVER)

OBSERVER
Captain America is one of the very cornerstones of Marvel Comics! When is Jack going to put Cap, charter member of the Avengers, back in the "real" world of the Marvel Universe, not fighting a cast of unknown aliens in a way-out science fiction future Earth.

(Lights shift to JACK)

JACK
The true test of heroism is making it on your own. There's strength in it, and that strength comes out in

what you do. That said, the reason I'm back is because I wanted to be back. I'm home. The people of Marvel are good people. They're cooperative.

(Lights shift again to OBSERVER, who adjusts his tape-repaired glasses)

OBSERVER
The last page or two of a Kirby book feels rushed and forced, like I've only read half a comic! I love Jack's art! Please, please chain him to the drawing board, make him draw every Marvel Comic, but keep him away from the typewriter!

(The OBSERVER exits. JACK slams down his pencil. And launches himself toward STAN)

JACK
You're kneecapping me with these letters! The reader picks up a book with all these knock letters, and figures the book ain't so good.

STAN
We publish your books! Why would we want to make you look bad?

JACK
You made those letters up when we started, why would you stop now?

STAN
Jack, I'm not the editor anymore! I don't pick the letters. They have me out in Hollywood trying to get movies and TV shows off the ground.

JACK
I still see your name plastered all over the books.

STAN
Honestly, Jack...I'm the publisher now. If you have a

problem with the editorial direction, talk to the Editor in Chief.

JACK
No one does anything around here without Stanley Lieber signing off! I want you to take the guys who are scheming to kill my books, and fire them!

STAN
Who?

JACK
You know damn well who!

STAN
I'm afraid I don't, Jack.

JACK
The hell you don't! I don't mind competition, but I want it to be fair.

STAN
Marvel lives and dies on its fans, you know that! I've spent fifteen years building this loyalty, and I'm telling you...

JACK
I hear the stories, how your editors make fun of my books. They're picking out the knock letters!

STAN
I understand how you feel. Nobody likes critics, but the readers get the final say!

JACK
Well, then maybe I just quit!

STAN
Do you want me to respond to that as your friend, or your publisher?

JACK
As far as I'm concerned, Stanley, you've never been anything but my editor.

(Moment as that sinks in)

STAN
Fine, Jack...Then, as your publisher, I will tell you this, Marvel Comics, a division of Cadence Industries, has a contract with you that demands a certain number of pages. A number you have not reached.

JACK
What are you going to do? Sue me?

STAN
Not me. I don't have a horse in this race...

JACK
Right, right! So you keep telling me.

STAN
But, I can assure you, Cadence WILL sue you.

JACK
Let 'em!

STAN
I don't think that's gonna help you get your art back.

(Beat)

JACK
God damn all you people. Thieves.

STAN
As. Your. Friend. And, no matter what you think, I've always thought of you that way...You belong here. You and I started all of this.

JACK
I did. You just slapped your name on it.

STAN
Obviously, that's how you see it. But, Jack, I am trying to help you.

JACK
The Silver Surfer thing?

STAN
They want it for a movie! This producer wants it for his girlfriend, Olivia Newton John!

JACK
Who the hell is that?

STAN
Some sort of singer, I think...Just like in the old days! We do this Silver Surfer book, and blow everyone's minds! C'mon, Jackson! One last time, you and me!

JACK
You and me, huh?

STAN
We'll get a piece of the film. We're setting up some animation work, and I can get you in there, too. All of it will go towards your contract.

(Beat)

JACK
This is the last time, Stanley.

STAN
I wish you didn't feel that way, Jack, but..if that's what you want.

JACK
I want done with this damn business, AND you.

(Projected: THE SILVER SURFER: THE ULTIMATE COSMIC EXPERIENCE cover)

(Lights shift. STAN steps out and addresses the reader)

STAN

Jolly Jack and I have created a cadre of crazy characters in collaboration during our years in the Marvel bullpen, but it's the Silver Surfer that dwells deepest in our ever-hammering hearts. And I can assure you, oh faithful friends of ol' Marvel, this is a masterpiece of Jack's awe-inspiring, eruptive artwork...and you won't find it on newsstands, oh no! It's at your local BOOKstore, true believer! Excelsior!

Scene Nine

(Lights shift, ROZ enters, clutching a cup of coffee)

ROZ
There used to be a time, every weekend, we'd have people come right into the driveway! I remember there was a family in a Winnebago. "Is this Jack Kirby's home? We just were driving through and wanted to shake Jack's hand." It was ninety degrees outside, so I told them to come in. I gave them cold drinks, and I told the kids to use the pool!

(She laughs and sips her coffee)

ROZ
The mother says, "I can't believe this, you're just like regular people!" I mean, this is Thousand Oaks. We're not Hollywood here! Pretty soon, Jack'd start telling his war stories. I'd walk out of the room...I'd heard them a million times! I finally told Kirby, God love 'em, but they have to call first.

(Another laugh. Lights shift, ROZ exits)

(Projected: Los Angeles — 1984)

(STAN and JOAN sit at a desk, waiting. He checks his watch, straightens his tie)

JOAN
Don't be nervous, they can smell fear.

STAN
I'm not nervous. Did you see that videotape they sent over?

JOAN
I am not going to watch something called "Revenge of the Ninja."

STAN
I should've listened to you.

JOAN
Well, he doesn't have bad taste. That's a Deganello over there.

STAN
Diagonal? Good name for it.

(MENAHEM GOLAN, an Israeli schlock movie producer who speaks in a heavy accent, bursts into the room)

GOLAN
Stan Lee! An honor to have you in my office! The Man!

(STAN jumps up)

(Projected: The Cannon Films Logo)

STAN
Mister Golan, let me tell you, the honor is all mine! It's so exciting to know that Marvel has found such a great partner for these films...

(The men shake hands)

GOLAN
Please, please...Call me Menahem. *(Notices JOAN)* Oh my! You didn't need to bring a pretty girl to get on my good side.

STAN
Well, I didn't.

JOAN
Bite your tongue, Stan!

STAN
This is my wife Joan.

GOLAN
(Taking her hand) If your husband is so foolish, perhaps you have dinner with me.

JOAN
(Laughing) I just love your office Menahem. Those Cassina chairs over there are divine!

GOLAN
Crap. My secretary got them. Make my ass sore.

JOAN
Oh! Well...

GOLAN
Straight business! I buy this...comedy book of yours, and I already have writers.

STAN
Well, that's just wonderful news! Marvel Productions has been doing pretty well with the animation...

GOLAN
Cartoons!?! Who gives two shits about cartoons? Cannon Films makes real movies! Captain America and Man-Spider.

STAN
Well, it's Spider-Man...

(Projected: Cannon Films Spider-Man trade ad)

GOLAN
My people tell me that we need you to sign off on scripts for good will. Two of my best guys banging on typewriters. Script in four weeks, tops!

JOAN
You know, Menahem, Stan here could write a smashing script for you.

GOLAN
You write?

JOAN
Stan has written literally thousands of comic books.

GOLAN
No, no! I need a REAL writer. I got great guy. Wrote "Radio K-KUM" and "Caught From Behind Two!" (Beat) Yeah, it's porn, but they're fast and cheap. You sign off, right now, and we get moving.

STAN
Well, I tell ya Menahem, the true believers..that's what I call our fans...have expectations.

GOLAN
Excellent! I love it! Truth believers! Now, first thing. We make sure to hit the trades. Full page! Cannon Pictures presents MAN-SPIDER! Boy bit by nuclear spider, becomes a monster! Kills everyone!

STAN
Menahem, I...Peter Parker is a hero.

(Beat)

GOLAN
Whatever! I'm not a story guy. Here!

(GOLAN *pulls out a Variety and flips to a full page ad for* Captain America)

(Projected: The Variety Captain America ad)

GOLAN
"Based on Stan Lee's Marvel comic strip character." You gotta like that!

JOAN
Oh! Isn't that just smashing, Stan?

STAN
Well, that's great, but I have to tell ya, I didn't create Cap.

GOLAN
"Cap?"

(STAN *picks up the Variety and points at the picture*)

STAN
Captain America. It was Jack...

GOLAN
Who cares! Cannon says you did! Listen Stanley...

(STAN *reacts to the name*)

GOLAN
In Hollywood? A guy's either a taxi driver, or a mogul. Up to you, but Cannon, and Golan, gonna make it happen!

(Lights shift to black)

(Projected: "Cannon Films Bankrupt" headline)

Scene Ten

(Lights shift in on JOAN, in direct address, martini in hand)

JOAN
All those kids see Stan as Marvel Comics. When Marvel was fighting with Jack Kirby over his artwork, they would blame Stan. You could never convince them that Stan is not Marvel. If Stan owned Marvel, we'd have a nicer house! I'm sure it bothered him, the artists not getting their artwork back. They were his friends. But he has a boss, too... *(Sips her drink)* You know I'm writing a novel now. Erotic fiction. "The Pleasure Palace." Stan's quite jealous.

(Lights shift. JOAN exits)

(Projected: The San Diego Comi-Con logo)

(JACK and ROZ sit at a table with JIM SHOOTER, the current Editor-in-Chief of Marvel Comics)

SHOOTER
Jack, I am so glad you and Roz could meet with me.

(Projected: July, 1985)

ROZ
Jim, Jack and I think you are good kid, but we've had it up to here with this.

SHOOTER
I'm here, as Marvel's current Editor-In-Chief, to try to resolve this situation.

JACK
Marvel has been jerkin' us around for years, Shooter!

SHOOTER
I certainly know how you feel, Jack. You too, Roz. It's why I asked the company to let me to speak with you here. No reason for you to fly all the way back to New York.

ROZ
We're too old for five and a half hour flights...

JACK
Both ways!

SHOOTER
Look, I know you want your art back, and the company would like to present eighty-eight pieces to you...as a gift...

JACK
A gift?!

SHOOTER
...in exchange for signing this document.

(SHOOTER produces several pages)

ROZ
There are literally thousands of pages of Jack Kirby art socked away someplace at Marvel.

SHOOTER
These are the pages we can account for.

(JACK *grabs the document and begins reading*)

ROZ
What happened to the rest of it?

SHOOTER
Roz, I promise you, we are looking.

ROZ
"Looking?" Those pages are the heart and soul of your whole company. I refuse to believe you just "lost them!"

JACK
This is a sack of garbage right here.

SHOOTER
It's a straightforward document.

JACK
Terminating my rights to the characters I created. I've seen the version other guys I worked with are getting. It's a half page!

SHOOTER
Jack, you have to understand yours is a special case.

(ROZ *takes the contract from* JACK)

JACK
What did Stanley sign?

SHOOTER
Stan has his own agreement.

JACK
Oh! Of course he does!

ROZ
It seems like Stanley owns everything.

SHOOTER
Roz, Stan doesn't own anything. He's got a contract for...

ROZ
He sure gets paid like it.

SHOOTER
Stan Lee is still employed by Marvel.

JACK
"Stan Lee presents" what does that mean?

SHOOTER
He's the publisher emeritus. It doesn't mean much, day-to-day, in terms of the books. Stan's heading Marvel Productions, mainly.

JACK
Goin' Hollywood. Funky Flashman to a T. I mean look at this!

(JACK pulls out the Cannon trade ad for Captain America)

(Projected: The Variety Captain America ad)

JACK
"Captain America – Based on Stan Lee's Marvel comic strip character!" Stanley Leiber was thirteen years old when Joe Simon and I created Captain America!

SHOOTER
That's Cannon Pictures, Jack. It's being corrected.

JACK
Stanley gets all the credit, 'cuz he's family.

SHOOTER
Martin Goodman sold Marvel eighteen years ago.

ROZ
The same thing over and over.

(*SHOOTER takes a breath*)

SHOOTER
Jack, you worked in packaging, ran a studio with Joe Simon.

JACK
Bet your ass I did.

SHOOTER
You self-published Mainline Comics in the fifties with Joe. You retained copyright on several characters, the Fighting American, for example. You employed dozens of artists to work under your byline. Correct?

JACK
I know what I did. What I accomplished.

SHOOTER
We all do. We all revere that work. Did you return art to any of those artists?

JACK
That was Joe Simon's deal.

ROZ
Jack didn't have anything to do with that.

SHOOTER
Jack, I know there's a lot of things in this document that seem unfair.

ROZ
It says he can't sell his original art! Why can John Buscema sell his pages, but Kirby can't?

SHOOTER
I know eighty-eight pages seems paltry.

JACK
Do you know how many pages I drew for Martin Goodman and Stanley Lieber?

SHOOTER
About thirteen thousand. Give or take.

ROZ
Exactly!

SHOOTER
I'll be straight with you, Roz. A whole lot of those are gone.

JACK
Gone?

SHOOTER
Given to fans, stolen, or...destroyed.

ROZ
From the beginning, Kirby wanted his art back. They said no, they were PRESERVING it in their warehouse! Jack always thought it was valuable, that his art was ART!

SHOOTER
Roz, you'll get no argument from me. You know that.

JACK
Don't shoot the messenger, baby.

SHOOTER
I swear to you, Roz, Jack, I personally have staff looking for more pages. We will find more, and if you sign this, it's going to go a long way toward greasing the wheels for me to return them, as well as a nice little pay-out for you.

(SHOOTER stands, revealing his imposing six foot, seven inch frame looming over the Kirbys)

SHOOTER
Please just sign it. For you, and your family.

JACK
You're the editor.

(Lights shift. ROZ and SHOOTER exit. JACK turns to the audience)

JACK
"I specifically retract, release, abandon and disclaim any rights to the copyright renewal term for 'Spider-Man,' 'The Incredible Hulk,' and 'The Fantastic Four' as alleged in my attorney's letter...I have reviewed the Writers and Artists Agreement between Marvel and myself, and I specifically acknowledge, confirm and reaffirm said agreements."

(Lights shift)

Scene Eleven

(Lights shift. We see ROBERT KNIGHT, *a handsome black radio host, sitting in his studio with* JACK*)*

(Projected: August 28th, 1987)

KNIGHT
Good morning, ladies and gentlemen, and welcome to Earthwatch, right here on WBAI in New York, I'm Robert Knight.

(Projected: The WBAI logo)

KNIGHT
Today we have a great treat for all of you, one of New York's native sons, in town from the sunny West Coast.

JACK
Warmer there, for sure.

KNIGHT
Got used to paradise, didn't you? Well, he may have abandoned us to the swimming pools and movie stars of California...

JACK
Riiight. Paul Newman's my pool boy.

KNIGHT
...But he's spending the morning with us here on WBAI to celebrate his 70th birthday. The King of Comics! Jack Kirby!

JACK
Happy to be here.

KNIGHT
Of course, we have to talk about the partnership with Stan Lee at Marvel Comics. Creating all these super heroes and dastardly villains...

JACK
To me, there are no villains, no heroes. I believe that people, when frustrated, will come into conflict with others, when inspired, they'll do things that transcend themselves. My stories are people stories, and there are elements that are very real.

KNIGHT
All those characters you were involved with; The Fantastic Four, The Hulk, Thor...So, what were those years like? The bullpen, the Merry Marvel Marching society, what was that like?

JACK
Well, it wasn't...it wasn't...well, I didn't consider it merry. The books sold, which was immensely satisfying. I considered it very...in those days being a professional was the thing. You turned in your work, and you got your wages and you went home.

KNIGHT
To hear Stan tell it...

JACK

I hate to disappoint these kids that want it dramatized or glorified or glamorized. I created and analyzed a situation, panel-by-panel. All of it was mine. I did everything but put words in the balloons.

KNIGHT

But, Jack, what about these legends of you and Stan acting the stories out, jumping on desks...

JACK

Maybe after I shut the door and went home.

KNIGHT

(Laughs) Well, listen! We're going to open a very special surprise door this morning. A special guest on the phone. Your colleague in arms, Stan Lee!

(Lights up on STAN, on the phone)

KNIGHT

Good morning Stan!

STAN

This is a hell of a coincidence! I'm in New York on business, and tuned in the radio, and there's my ol' pal Jolly Jack celebrating his birthday! I couldn't let the occasion pass without picking up the phone and saying "many happy returns Jack!"

JACK

Well, Stanley, I want to thank you for calling. I hope you're in good health and stay in good health...

STAN

I'm doin' my best! And same to you! I just want to say, without getting too saccharine, that one of the marks of a great artist is having his own style. King Kirby had a style nobody has ever come close to, and you should be proud of it. And I'm proud of you for it.

JACK
Well...I do have to thank you for helping me keep and evolve that. I'm certain that, whatever we did together, we got sales for Marvel, and I...

STAN
It was more than that Jack! I guess who did what will be argued forever, but it was always more than the sum of its parts. There was magic when we worked together. I am very happy to have had that experience.

JACK
Well...I was never sorry for it. If the product was good, that was my satisfaction. I respect that you're certainly a good professional and fond of a good product. That's the mark of all of us.

STAN
You notice I never interrupt you when you're saying something nice about me.

KNIGHT
I'd like to put it to you gentlemen that what made your work so tremendous...It really doesn't matter, when it comes right down to it, who exactly did what. Although, I do have to say, as a fan, it would be interesting to know if Galactus' exit speech in Fantastic Four number fifty was Jack's dialogue or...

STAN
Every word of dialogue in those scripts was mine. Every story.

JACK
I wrote a few lines myself above every panel...

STAN
They weren't printed in the book!

KNIGHT
All right, look! Both of you...hey kids! Both of you guys...

(*The lights shift, The OBSERVER appears, and waves a hand*)

(*Projected: Another Kirby Krackle*)

(*STAN and JACK rise, aware of The OBSERVER and that they now share physical space*)

STAN
Jack, answer me truthfully, Did you ever read any of the stories after they were finished? I don't think you did!

JACK
I wasn't allowed to write...

STAN
You were always busy drawing the next one. You never read the finished book.

JACK
It was the action I was interested in.

STAN
That was clear! The same action you'd pumped out in thirty other books! How many patriotic heroes did you do? How many boy gangs? Kept going to back to the same well. Y'know what I gave you? Humanity!

JACK
Why I oughta paste you! All you ever did was steal credit for MY work!

STAN
When? When did I do that, Jack? When I called you the

King? When I plastered your name on every book we published? When I made "Stan and Jack" the core of the whole company's creative identity?

JACK
When you re-wrote history? Wiped me and Ditko out of it?

STAN
YOU QUIT! You quit TWICE! What was I supposed to do? "Hey, here's a genius that worked hand-in-hand with me to build the foundations of The House of Ideas, he's the best artist I've ever seen, and you should read ALL his stuff! But he's working for the Distinguished Competition...go buy their books?!"

JACK
Maybe I wouldn't have quit if you and Goddamn Martin Goodman treated me with a little respect. Crap money, holding my art hostage...

STAN
I had nothing to do with that!

JACK
The hell you didn't, Stanley!

STAN
WILL YOU STOP CALLING ME THAT!?!

(STAN takes a deep breath)

STAN
Nobody has more respect for you than me, Jack. You know that. I don't think you ever thought the dialogue was important. It's what you drew that mattered, and maybe you're right. I don't agree, but maybe you are.

(Beat. Both men regard each other)

STAN
Maybe I didn't stand up for you enough. Maybe I focused on myself too much. I am only a human being, just like you. You can be angry with me, you can be angry with Martin, you can be angry with Marvel, but for God's sake...can't you just agree that we worked really well together? Y'know, Jack...I don't care who owns what. I'd just like to work with you once more.

(Lights shift back as KNIGHT cuts back in)

KNIGHT
Gentlemen, what we're seeing here is part of the inner dynamics. You complimented each other, and held one another in check. A great product emerged, keeping greater attention to characters, to detail, to verisimilitude, than to the egos of the people creating them.

(The OBSERVER exits. STAN and JACK return to their seats)

JACK
I'm only trying to say the human being is important. It should come from an individual.

STAN
You know, when you mention the ego problem... The funny thing is, I think when we were working, we were just doing the best we could.

KNIGHT
Ego is the fuel of creativity.

STAN
Well, since it's Jack's birthday.

(Moment. STAN pulls out a sheet of paper and reads)

STAN
I just want to say that Jack "The King" Kirby has made

a tremendous mark on American, if not world, culture, and I think he should be incredibly proud and pleased with himself. I wish him, Roz and his family, all the best. I hope ten years from now, I'll be in a town somewhere listening to a tribute to his 80th birthday and have the opportunity to call and wish him well again.

(Moment. He stops reading)

STAN
Jack, I love ya.

(Beat. STAN hangs up, his light goes out)

JACK
Well, same here Stan, but...

(Moment. JACK realizes STAN has gone)

JACK
Thank you very much, Stan...Robert?

KNIGHT
Yes, Jack?

JACK
Yeah, listen. You can understand, now. How things really were.

(Moment)

JACK
I want to thank you for having me on your show, and your courtesy. It was pleasant to
talk to you.

(JACK gets up and walks out of the light. Lights fade to black)

Scene Twelve

(Projected: The San Diego Comi-Con logo)

(Lights up on The OBSERVER, his robes and affectation are gone, fully and completely human. He wears a t-shirt, reading "Stan and Jack," with "Jack and Stan" immediately below)

OBSERVER
I managed to find Jack in the throngs of the convention center. I was scared to death, as I asked for an autograph.

(Lights shift and JACK appears. He follows the OBSERVER's narration)

OBSERVER
Jack patted my arm, and asked what I had in my portfolio. When I said it was my samples, Jack lit up, and ordered me...

JACK
You want to be a pro? You can't hide that stuff kid! Let me see!

OBSERVER
I was showing him, when, out of nowhere, Stan came striding down the aisle.

(Lights shift and STAN appears. He and JACK shake hands, embrace and begin chatting and laughing silently)

OBSERVER
They warmly greeted each other, and were chatting like long-lost friends.

(The OBSERVER takes out his camera)

OBSERVER
I asked if I could get a picture.

STAN
What do you think, Jackson? A picture for our Merry Marvel Marcher here?

JACK
Just cool it with the rabbit ears, Stanley.

OBSERVER
That captured moment has stuck with me in the decades since. All the fighting, the fans who argue so vehemently and certainly about what happened all those years ago. The events no one can ever "prove." The anger and the ugly rhetoric. What would it say about us if, years after the men in front of me had left us, it was still raging?

(They laugh. STAN throws his arm around JACK, and both men smile warmly)

OBSERVER
Yet, as they stood there together oh so briefly... I knew that none of it, the mythology that had defined so much of my life, could exist if either one of them had not brought the best of themselves onto those pages.

STAN
Say EXCELSIOR!

JACK
Always gotta get the last word, don't ya?

(They laugh. Flashbulb. Lights smash to black)

(Projected: The final photo of STAN and JACK)

END OF PLAY

About the Playwright

Mark Pracht was raised in the mountains near Colorado Springs, Colorado. He is Alumni of the University of Nebraska, Kearney, and was a company member of the Sheleterbelt Theatre in Omaha, Nebraska. During that time, he helped develop and produce seven world premiere productions, including his own full-length play, *NEON*.

He's worked as an actor, director and playwright in the Chicago theatre community since 2001, and received the 2019 Joseph Jefferson Award for Best Performance in a Principal Role for his portrayal of Harlan "Mountain" McClintock in Rod Serling's *Requiem for a Heavyweight* at The Artist Home theatre.

His work has been produced in Chicago by Brown Couch Theatre company, where he served as Artistic Director, and Strangeloop theatre.

MORE PLAYS
ON SALE NOW FROM
SORDELET INK
WWW.SORDELETINK.COM

ACTION MOVIE: THE PLAY
JOE FOUST & RICHARD RAGSDALE

You want a play with a car chase, an alligator attack, and a bunch of super-cool fight scenes? Hoo boy, have we got something for you! When wiseacre supervillain John Kreegar gets his filthy mitts on an eldritch artifact of terrible power, everybody's ass is up for grabs! Luckily, the mysterious Dr. Xylene is putting together a fantastic team of good guys to fix Kreegar's wagon but good!

ALL CHILDISH THINGS
JOSEPH ZETTELMAIER

A heist comedy to warm the hearts of Star Wars fans! Dave Bullanski is planning the greatest heist ever. The idea is to take over an old Kenner warehouse and clean out all the rare Star Wars memorabilia, selling it off to a private collector willing to spend $2 million for the loot.

CAMPFIRE
JOSEPH ZETTELMAIER

A horror play. Marcus Carver has brought his niece and nephew back home. In the woods behind his farm, around a campfire, the Carvers will tell stories as they have for many generations. But a stranger has entered the dimly-lit circle.

CAPTAIN BLOOD
DAVID RICE

Unjustly sentenced to slavery on a Caribbean island, the bold Dr. Peter Blood falls in love with the lady of the plantation, the lovely Arabella Bishop. When Blood escapes and takes up the life of a pirate, it appears that fate has separated them forever…or has it? Filled with sword fights and pirate battles, love and treachery, and even a song or two, Captain Blood is a pirate adventure perfect for the whole crew!

CHURCHILL
RONALD KEATON

March 1946. After leading Britain and her Allies to victory in the European Theatre, Winston Churchill has been shockingly defeated for re-election as Prime Minister. Living in forced retirement, Churchill receives an invitation from President Harry Truman to speak at Westminster College in Fulton, Missouri, where he will deliver his legendary, emphatic "Iron Curtain" speech.

THE COUNT OF MONTE CRISTO
CHRISTOPHER M. WALSH

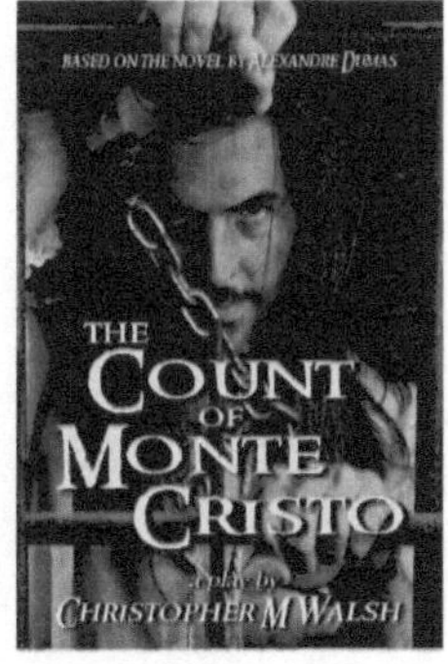

Framed by a conspiracy and torn from the woman he loves, Edmond Dantes is wrongly imprisoned for fourteen years. Escaping captivity, he enters the upper reaches of Parisian society, insinuating himself into the lives of his three tormentors as, one by one, he seeks to use their own secrets to destroy them in the guise of his new identity: the Count of Monte Cristo. A dark tale of intrigue and vengeance by epic storyteller Alexandre Dumas.

THE DECADE DANCE
JOSEPH ZETTELMAIER

A one-night stand becomes a ten-year journey as Rog and Nina navigate a relationship against the backdrop of a turbulent decade. A touching two-hander, carefully balancing nostalgia, romance, and humor as two people live unexpected lives.

DEAD MAN'S SHOES

Joseph Zettelmaier

A dark and hilarious western, with a dash of buddy-comedy. Notorious outlaw Injun Bill Picote has escaped from prison, along with a hard-luck drunk named Froggy. The unlikely partners endure trials and bizarre misadventures as they set out to right a terrible wrong.

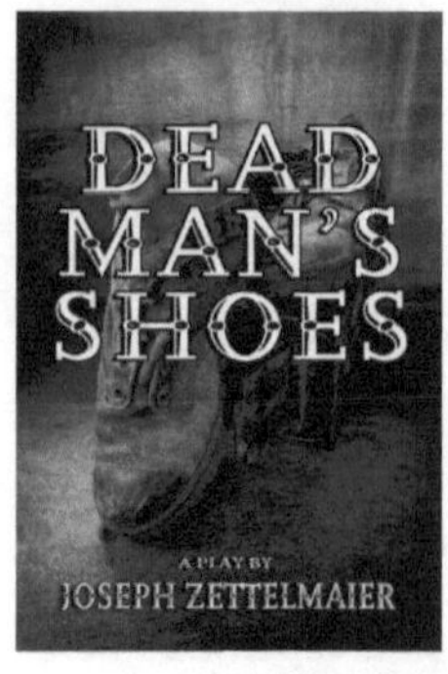

DR. SEWARD'S DRACULA

Joseph Zettelmaier

Dr. Seward has cut himself off from the rest of the world after losing his lover and friends to Dracula. The Irish author Bram Stoker wishes to tell his story. Soon, a series of murders occur, very similar to the ones Seward fought to stop. A re-imagining of Bram Stoker's *Dracula*.

EBENEZER: A Christmas Play

Joseph Zettelmaier

It's a cold Christmas Eve in London, and Ebenezer Scrooge sits in a hospital room. 15 years have passed since his miraculous transformation by the Ghosts of Christmas. They are about to return for a final judgment. Based on Charles Dickens' classic *A Christmas Carol*.

Eve of Ides

David Blixt

The night before his assassination at the hands of conspirators, Julius Caesar attended a feast. With him were Brutus, Cassius, and Antony. During the meal, Caesar was asked what he thought was the best way to die. Caesar answered, 'What does it matter, so long as it's quick?' Based on history and the works of Shakespeare, Eve Of Ides reveals the unexplored relationship between the main players of the age — Caesar, Brutus, and Antony.

FRANKENSTEIN
ROBERT KAUZLARIC

When an unexpected death shatters her family, Victoria retreats into the darkest recesses of her psyche in search of a way forward. To find meaning in this impossible loss, she brings a terrible creation to life — one whose existence threatens all hopes for the future. Haunted and hunted at every turn, Victoria must endure a nightmare journey of the soul in a quest for survival. A brilliant reimagining of the 1818 thriller by Mary Wollstonecraft Shelley.

HAUNTED
JOSEPH ZETTELMAIER

"The best way to know a place is through its ghosts." Michigan playwright Joseph Zettelmaier set out to collect a wide variety of ghost stories for this anthology play of true otherworldly encounters by Michiganders from Milan to Marquette.

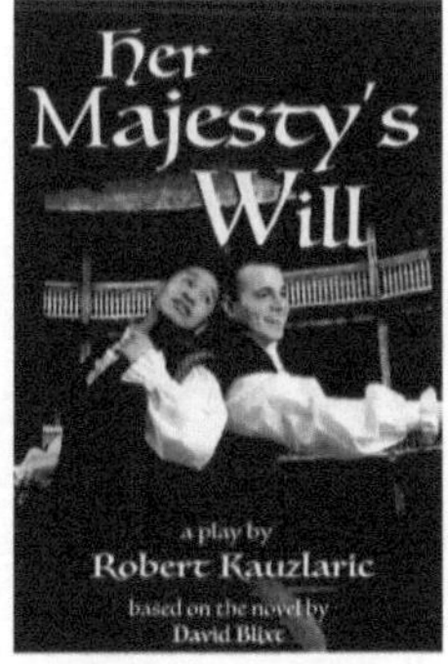

HER MAJESTY'S WILL
ROBERT KAUZLARIC

Young William Shakespeare is hiding from the law in rural Lancashire, languishing as a simple school master. Christopher Marlowe is living the high life as a spy for the Crown. When a dastardly plot to assassinate the Queen draws these two unforgettable wits together, Will is swept up in a world of intrigue, treachery, and mayhem in an adventure that will define the rest of his life — if he can only manage to survive it.

IT CAME FROM MARS
JOSEPH ZETTELMAIER

A hilarious look at the night of Orson Welles' famous *War Of The Worlds* broadcast! The members of Farlowe's Mystery Theatre Hour are in rehearsal for their weekly radio show when they hear an alarming announcement come over the radio—Martians have landed! Suddenly secrets are revealed as the cast and crew believe it is their last night on earth!

THE JIGSAW BRIDE

JOSEPH ZETTELMAIER

A century after Victor Frankenstein's demise, the brilliant scientist Maria von Moos unearths his secrets when she stumbles upon a mesmerizing discovery — Justine, a woman frozen in time. Maria brings Justine into her home, setting the stage for a captivating odyssey of science and hope.

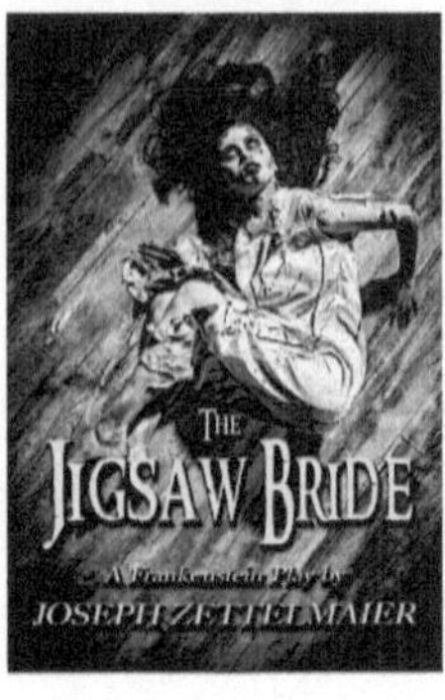

THE LEAGUE OF AWESOME

CORRBETTE PASKO & SARA SEVIGNY

The superheroes of The League Of Awesome have done it again. They decided to punish the SorrowMaker by trapping him inside a Hardy Boys book. Yeah, it was a little unconventional. Zoe, Sylvia, Penny, Kitty & Rumble wouldn't let him escape. I mean....come on! They'd have to be drunk to do that! Now let's watch them celebrate their victory over him with mojitos. Oh...oh dear.

MALAPERT LOVE

SIAH BERLATSKY

A hilarious mash-up/homage/reimagining of classical comedic elements! *Malapert Love* is a modern response to the tropes, style and structure of Shakespeare's comedies. It follows the tangled and farcical action of a group of people who have all fallen in love with the wrong person.

THE MAN-BEAST

JOSEPH ZETTELMAIER

The wilds of France are stalked by a fearsome creature—the Beast of Gévaudan. An outcast forester presents its corpse to King Louis for a rich reward. However, the story he told may not have been the entire truth. Based on the legends of the loupe-garou, the famous French warewolf.

THE MAN WHO WAS THURSDAY
BILAL DARDAI

When Gabriel Syme joins the undercover detail tasked with infiltrating an anarchists' operations, he soon finds himself sitting on their Supreme Council with the code name "Thursday." It slowly becomes clear that no one in this battle between law and chaos is as they seem — and that Scotland Yard may have created the very problem they're trying to solve. Uncover the truth in this absorbing adaptation of the 1908 satire by G. K. Chesterton.

THE MOONSTONE
ROBERT KAUZLARIC

The Moonstone, an Indian diamond steeped in a history of violence and mysticism, is stolen from Rachel Verinder's sitting room, and no one in her household is above suspicion. Join an unforgettable collection of liars, lovers, addicts and outcasts as they struggle to uncover the truth and reclaim the stone before its curse destroys them all. This thrilling mystery by Wilkie Collins is regarded as the first detective novel in the English language.

ONCE A PONZI TIME
JOE FOUST

For years, Harold has 'helped' his friends with their investments, but his artful dodging and shady shenanigans are about to collapse around him as his pyramid scheme tumbles to earth. With only the help of his flakey father, his naive nephew, and a ventriloquist's dummy, can Harold hoodwink the Russian mob, bamboozle the SEC, and restore his friends' fortunes without his entire world becoming a complete farce? Watch him try!

THE SCULLERY MAID
JOSEPH ZETTELMAIER

Having declared an uneasy truce in England's ongoing war with France, King Edward III and his nobles celebrate in Nottingham Castle. Unbeknownst to the king, a murder plot is being hatched in the kitchen by the lowliest of his servants, who seeks revenge to right the wrongs of a lifetime. Religion, politics, and questions of loyalty, all at a knife's edge.

ANTON CHEKHOV'S THE SEAGULL
JANICE L. BLIXT & ALEXANDRA LaCOMBE

This new translation of Anton Chekhov's classic The Seagull restores what most English-language versions of the play omit: humor. Considered a world-class humorist and wit, Chekov intended this play to be a Comedy. Translated by Alexandra LaCombe and adapted by award-winning director Janice L. Blixt, this is The Seagull audiences have been waiting for.

SEASON ON THE LINE
SHAWN PFAUTSCH

A novice assistant stage manager joins the crew of Bad Settlement Theatre Company for their make-or-break season. An aging artistic director is hell-bent on mounting the elusive perfect staging of Moby Dick. The play swings from soliloquy to action-adventure story as the young man grows to love the theatrical live, even a those around him pay the ultimate price for their pursuit of theatre's own great white whale.

A TALE OF TWO CITIES
CHRISTOPHER M. WALSH

The Reign of Terror sweeps through Paris, and two Londoners are confronted with impossible choices. Will aristocratic Charles Darnay abandon his family to protect an innocent man? Can depressive barrister Sydney Carton make the ultimate sacrifice for unrequited love? An epic story of resurrection and redemption, based on the 1859 novel by Charles Dickens.

VOICES IN THE DARK
JOSEPH ZETTELMAIER

Turn out the lights and shiver with delight at this anthology collection of seven short horror radio plays by renowned horror writer Joseph Zettelmaier.

OTHER WORKS FROM
SORDELET INK
WWW.SORDELETINK.COM

HOLD, PLEASE
STAGE MANAGING A PANDEMIC
RICHARD HESTER

A pandemic chronicle from the particular point of view of a career Broadway stage manager living in Manhattan. Part journal, part blog, these essays attempted to make sense of the crisis and what it was doing to us. By the end, everything had changed. What follows is a journey through one of the most fascinating periods in both our cultural and our personal histories.

NELLIE BLY'S WORLD
VOL. 1 - III

EDITED BY DAVID BLIXT

Bly's complete reporting, collected for the very first time! Starting with the stunt that made hers a household name, Nellie Bly spends her first year at the New York World going undercover to expose frauds, sharpsters and boodlers, interviewing Belva Lockwood and Hangman Joe, and traveling around the world!

THE MASTER OF VERONA

Cangrande della Scala is everything a man should be. Daring. Charming. Ruthless. To the poet Dante, he is the ideal Renaissance prince—until Dante's son discovers a secret that could be Cangrande's undoing. Thrust into the betrayal surrounding Verona's prince, Pietro Alighieri must navigate a rivalry that severs a friendship, divides a city, and sparks a feud that will produce Shakespeare's famous star-crossed lovers, Romeo & Juliet.